The Mystery of Salt Marsh House

S.H.Keen

ISBN 978-1-7393559-0-6

www.enchantedengland.co.uk

Cover design by: Sarah Keen

Foreword

Thank you for taking the time to read Salt Marsh House. It has been a long time in the making. Commander Ebb entered my life in the early 2000s and dictated the first third of this story. He then, unhelpfully, stopped. It had such dark themes that I put the notebook in a drawer but he would not go away and was insistent I helped finish his story. Consequently, in2013, I studied for a creative and critical MA with Winchester University. They gave me the tools to unpick his history and give it shape. I am grateful to University tutors, Mark Rutter and Carole Burns who nurtured my writing. Gaining an M.A has been life changing and life enhancing Thank you too to my many friends who read early drafts and for their thoughtful and constructive feedback.

To my father

Corris Geoffrey Keen

The battle was won but the war was lost, though at this late hour the men did not know it, and their HQ did not tell them as they made their triumphant entry into the defeated town.

Commander Charles Ebb requisitioned a tank and drove it down the high street, enjoying the bombed buildings that swayed around him. Ruined houses gave poor cover to the weak and the homeless who had failed to get out in time. The invading battalion joyfully hunted them down. Strange cries rang from the side streets and dark alleyways.

It was evening when Commander Ebb reached the Hotel de Ville that was reported to be damaged but still standing. His unit's weapons had machined-gunned the town into a sullen peace and it was here he had planned to set up their headquarters and manage the defeated region. His task was *to maintain martial law until further orders.*

These staccato instructions beating down over the damaged wires had said no more and officers, on their receipt, had not commented.

The Hotel de Ville had survived the worst of the town's destruction and functioned as the army's new headquarters but it's desecrated rooms gave little shelter. After a week, Commander Ebb decided he could do better. He instructed his batman to find suitable accommodation.

The batman was a precise man, a thin man who wanted to grow fat – *'and will do,'* he said to himself, 'when *this is over*'. The batman promised himself many things: food and ease were high on his list.

The troops nicknamed him *The Bagman* and laughed at the clicking and clinking that could be heard from his rucksack's countless pockets; it was a coded sound caused by tiny sums of money that the Bagman had taken from the many ruins or abandoned corpses the army had come across.

The first time the Bagman heard his nickname a slow, sharp smile crossed his face. He looked up at his comrades who lounged on some steps above and around him. 'The dead don't need the money,' he said. 'I never killed them for it. I just took what I found.' This truth he placed on the stairs that he rested on. At this level, it was not challenged by his cynical and amused listeners.

The Bagman was conscientious in his hunt for a suitable house. He searched many thoroughly. He returned later the same afternoon and unfurled a map as he briefed Commander Ebb.

'There is a fine country house here, Sir—Salt Marsh House. It can be well defended and is close to town.' The Bagman paused. 'But there is something, Sir, it was owned by a Mme Stutzman. But no one has seen her since the town fell.'

Commander Ebb stared at him.

'I plan to take the house, not rent it,' he informed his Bagman. 'If the woman has left—so much the easier for us.'

The Bagman gazed at him levelly and continued. 'There is something odd Sir. The remaining people would hardly discuss her at all. No trace of servants fled or dead. And the house is secret somehow.'

Commander Ebb was sharp. He had no use or time for enigmas unless they were of a military kind. 'Secret or not, we move in tonight.'

It was late; an hour from dawn by the time Commander Ebb drove through the vast iron gates and long drive of Salt Marsh House. The moon had set and the morning star hung above his head.

Salt Marsh House lay before him; unresolved in the darkness.

His bagman met him at the door and led him through the main entrance.

'Sir, this way. Thorough check, no power, no food, no water, no-one.'

The Bagman spoke the truth as he saw it. He led the Commander through a dark hall and up a vast, shadowy staircase. Their boots beat out a staccato message that rang through the house.

– .–. ..– – ....

Finally, the Bagman opened a door into a luxuriously furnished bedroom. An antique mahogany bed stood upon on a finely woven Persian rug. A chest of drawers had been richly decorated with red and ebony lacquer in CHINOISORIE style. It held a dark landscape. Golden birds scurried through finely painted leaves and grasses that stretched across a black and gleaming marsh. At its shore, it was possible to glimpse a woman. She stood at the door of her house whilst holding open a magnificent fan that shielded her face from view.

Commander Ebb entered, closed the door behind him and fell instantly asleep on the bed. The long day was over at last.

The next morning brought the news Commander Ebb was expecting. He was to hold onto the town and keep it quiet. In truth, there was nowhere else for either him or the army to go.

Commander Ebb worked ruthlessly to restore order and supplies to the town. Justice was something else; that he did not believe in. He imposed his martial law —justice lay in the hands of the future or God. The Commander washed his hands of the women, the children, the weak. The girls of his youth had been a torment with their mad passions and teasing letters. In the end, they bored him and he lived, he found, very well without them. He looked after the town's supply chain, paid informers and something like peace or method returned. Once the provisions were in place, he reasoned vaguely to those around him who raised the subject, the fortunes of the weak would also improve. He did not stay in the town to see the result of this theory. Each evening he returned to Salt March House but it was some days before he explored it, many more before he began to realise just what it was the house held.

Commander Ebb woke one morning and reviewed his achievements. A rare satisfaction filled him. This was, he judged, well earned; the battle won, the town quiet, his army orderly and reaping its reward from the area. No new orders had come through from any higher authority, and anyway—he imagined—he worked better without a directive.

Dawn

.- -. .-

Early morning sunlight filtered through the shuttered windows as dawn broke. Commander Ebb rose from his bed and opened them, to reveal a bright landscape and a fine estate of trees and grounds. A large scorch mark was burnt into the lawn but other than that it had escaped, it seemed, the recent ugly battle. He adjusted the shutters so the light slanted its rays like lances across the wooden floor.

The Bagman appeared. 'Breakfast Sir, Coffee.' The Bagman was meticulous in his preparation. 'Sir, reminding you I am off today. Have some business to take care of, Sir. I have left food in the kitchen along with supplies.'

Commander Ebb stared. He had only a vague recollection of this arrangement

'Good God man. Find me a replacement—some domestic. Haven't you organised one already?'

The Bagman returned his look. 'With respect, Sir, no one from the town will stay here. Flatly refuse to come, Sir—not even for money.'

Commander Ebb refused to ask why. He was almost too irritated to speak.

'Second a private. Dear God!' he exclaimed.

The Bagman agreed and left. In his heart, he was glad to be leaving although he could not know why.

Commander Ebb watched the Bagman disappear. It would be sometime before his replacement could arrive. It was unlike the Bagman, Commander Ebb thought, to foul up like that.

He poured another coffee and lounged back on his bed. Despite himself, the unaccustomed quietness was washing over him, lulling him into a daze. Later, looking back, he never could remember how much time he had spent in this trance-like state. Not long, judging by the position of the sun. But what he did know, when he started awake, reaching with a catlike agility for his gun—he knew with a military certainty; somebody was observing him within that seeming empty room. He called out but an utter silence greeted him. Nothing, not even birdsong filled the space.

Morning

.- -. .-

Commander Ebb fastened his gun to his holster and walked out; his sharp senses were alert. He would find what he sought—of that he was certain. The Commander walked from the room and ran lightly down the stairs and into the grounds. Once there he turned and surveyed the land.

The Bagman had not lied when he reported on the house's isolation but had not pushed his enquiries too far. The house was there, the house was suitable and therefore he did not trouble himself further.

Commander Ebb returned to the house and slowly moved through the ground floor. He pulled open long shutters and saw rooms sharpen into focus. They were still furnished as though waiting for their owner to return. The walls, however, showed lighter areas, displaying lost paintings.

They had only recently been removed,

Commander Ebb realised. Small spills of plaster still lay on the floors where hooks had been wrenched out. *Unhappy house,* thought Commander Ebb and shivered. Why would he think that? The house was abandoned, that was all.

Commander Ebb finished his tour of the grounds. He could see that an earlier version of Salt Marsh House had been remodelled into a classical style, its exterior walls were redressed in white stone with columns added to the main entrance and hall. Inside there were hints to its original structure—a confused selection of abruptly terminated walls, of unexpected spaces and oddly shaped cupboards. It was a luxurious and once loved house. A great staircase linked the floors at the front of the house. At the back, several small stairways allowed the servants to reach the grand rooms without being seen.

Four vast reception rooms occupied most of

house's centre and then, at the back, a cluster of older rooms; pantries, larders, closets, kitchens all, apart from the Bagman's rudimentary kit, devoid of artefacts. A cellar had been hastily emptied of its contents, a broken crate still lay oozing a sticky mess on the steps. Commander Ebb cursed and then returned to the jumbled assortment of rooms.

He studied the angles and sections of the walls. *Somewhere,* he thought, *somewhere I will find you.* But he did not ask this time why he thought that or what he sought.

Commander Ebb went out of the house and studied the back elevation. Here, most clearly you could trace the old medieval roof of the house and, he realised, the hotchpotch collection of kitchens and cupboards did not use all the space that the house made available to them. There was unallocated space within.

He returned to the cool and whitewashed

interior of the main kitchen and stood in the shaded doorway, studying the room. Sunlight picked out his face in chiaroscuro; his body, to an invisible watcher, remained hidden—dark.

Commander Ebb counted the series of tiny, diamond lattice windows across the wall. One, two, three, four—a balanced number that stopped elegantly before a set of oak shelves. They were lime-washed and solidly built from floor to ceiling. He remembered the sequence from outside the house: five. He was certain there were five. The last hidden behind the creeping ivy that was laying claim to Salt Marsh House.

He started to work his way through the lengths of shelves.

Tap, tap, tap, as insistent as orders, the rhythm of his body knocked out a steady sound.

– .–. ..– – ....

He worked his way along the wall until the sound from the plaster changed to a hollow dull thud. Commander Ebb was not a man to rush. Methodically he sought and found some tools from an outhouse. Carefully he returned and dismantled a section of shelving. Once these were down he started on the plaster and there, sure enough, as he beat down the plaster coverings, a door slowly revealed itself. He rubbed down the corroded hinges and oiled them. Finally, he found a nail and used it to lift the latch.

Whoever had covered the entrance had expected the disguise to work; the door was not locked or fixed. A surprisingly small push gave Commander Ebb access to the interior.

He stumbled therefore into a dark chamber and he cursed himself. He had forgotten his army regular torch. He forced the door wide open in the hope that the sunlight in the kitchen would illuminate him further. But he remained, shadowy in the unknown. He steadied his breath and waited for his eyes to adjust.

Gradually he saw he was in a square chamber, an ornate stone fireplace broke up one stretch of wall. A mirror was set above the mantelpiece. The room was richly decorated. Some of the walls were lined with books, their spines glinting with gold.

On the largest wall hung beautifully woven and embroidered tapestries. In them Commander Ebb could see a gleam of crowns and a flash of jewels as silken kings rode through spun thickets. A wool kilim carpet covered a flag stoned floor. Strangely—apart from the disturbance caused by

Commander Ebb—there was, he noticed, no dust, nothing to indicate any passage of time.

In the centre of the room stood a small circular table and on it lay an open book. As Commander Ebb drew near he could see it was a notebook and on it, in a black and sharply written hand, was written:

'Help Me'

At the same moment that Commander Ebb read this, a great cry echoed through Salt Marsh House. The call was repeated, drawing closer through the sunlit rooms. In his dark chamber, Commander Ebb gasped, cursed and then marched back into the bright kitchen.

He was just in time to prevent the Private entering. The Private stopped helloing abruptly. He saw Commander Ebb's face.

'Reporting, Sir. I am sorry, Sir, the Bagman forgot to remind me, Sir. I am late, Sir.'

This man is lying, thought Commander Ebb. *This man is lying. What was he saying*?

'Nice place, Sir, fine house,' the Private continued, hoping to avoid an oncoming storm.

Commander Ebb hustled him out.

'Not here Private! Not here. This room...' Commander Ebb fought for the word. 'This room is *mine*.'

The Private backed away. 'Sir, fine Sir. I'll use the pantry. I'll set my kit up, get a brew on.'

He turned into the pantry and started work. 'No problem Sir.'

Commander Ebb closed the kitchen door behind him and locked it. Then he made his way outside into the hot day.

The heat made Commander Ebb pause about crossing the wide lawn to the cool woods beyond. He was breathing deeply and felt exhilarated, exactly as when he fought his battles, the joy of winning.

The Private came out and served up his brew of coffee. 'Everything alright, Sir? Good, Sir.' He did not stay to hear a reply.

Commander Ebb neither heard nor saw him. He thought he saw on the edge of the lawn a slight, light figure, observed and then gone. He shouted for the Private who came running.

He denied all knowledge of anyone in the grounds and reluctantly followed Commander Ebb to check the woods.

'Nothing Sir, not even phantoms,' he grumbled to himself and took a drink from his hip flask. He had been in Salt Marsh House for less than an hour and he felt boredom creeping into his bones. No one was going to attack Commander Ebb and cooking was for women. At headquarters the whole command was waiting for orders that never arrived. No-one came or went. He took another drink and felt the resentment fester.

They had been well and truly stitched up, the Private reasoned, by high and mighty officers —betrayed by their weak command into enemy hands. He had fought so hard, delivered so much and all for nothing.

The Private brooded and soon was in a mood for mischief. He returned to the small pantry and unloaded his standard military transmitter. His discontented requests were turned by the machine into a rapid tittle-tattle of staccato noise. Unknown to the Private, the house heard

•– •• •• • •••

and carried them on. Its whispers flowed out of the house, along ancient pathways to the horizon, mingling with the reeds and the marsh grasses, disturbing old wrongs and rousing old listeners from their restless sleep.

Commander Ebb returned to the cool interior of Salt Marsh House; the Private paused the singing notes of his malice until the Commander unlocked the door and passed through into the unseen chamber.

Commander Ebb crossed to the table and re-opened the book he found earlier.

'Help Me'

Apart from this, the book was empty. The fine lines of black ink held the one imperative. It was all that could be read. Commander Ebb turned the pages carefully and held them up against the light. Nothing faded; nothing once committed and now lost. Looking out of the window he saw the

Private stalking across the lawn. Black against the bright green: his dark shadow cast before him as the morning sun started its ascent into the sky.

Commander Ebb turned back into the little chamber: *help me.* The words started to beat into his brain. The room was unchanged, quiet, clean and cool. He steadied his breath. The books remained unopened on their shelves. The chimney place was free from ash and only old, cold soot clung to the fireback. *Could there be more little rooms,* he wondered. In his mind's eye, he saw the exterior of the house and knew the remaining divisions matched the external frame.

For the first time, Commander Ebb felt alone. In a slight panic, he re-opened the book and in a scrawled hand wrote:

How?

He sat down by the fireplace and lit a cigarette. Suddenly he remembered his mother who told him of the secret people. It was a sharp, unlocked memory, for she had died young and become one of the secret people herself.

The Private paced restlessly outside the house, panting in the heat. He waited expectantly the result of his message. He knew the town better than most—better than many locals in fact. He was a good hunter. He knew how to enjoy himself in the worst of circumstances and these circumstances were not bad at all. He started into the house and counted the rooms. He returned to the garden where he too scrutinised the old house's structure. He calculated and he *knew.* Then he smiled. The Private pulled out his cigarette paper and an ample twist of tobacco. His match flared briefly and the first plumes of smoke drifted across the lawn.

Commander Ebb went to the window and

opened it, pushing back into the ivy and myriad creeping plants that tied the frames back to the house. He could smell the Private's smoke. Commander Ebb peered again at the shadows that edged the lawn. He looked for the white figure; but he was sure now there was no one.

He sighed, turned and leaned against the window frame. He had no orders, he reflected. There was still no word from HQ and now in this room he gave way to a curious sensation that there was no HQ and perhaps never had been. He considered who had governed his life's actions up to this point.

He had received orders; that was certain. They had arrived in proper forms of memos, papers or drummed down the always inadequate lines of communications. But now he wondered from whence they came and who had given them. The house pressed around him and he was aware once more of its great silence. The notion grew on him that if he were to open the door of the room now, it would not lead to the kitchen and the great hall, but to something unknown.

He wondered too, if he opened the door, whether he would not see another version of himself in another hidden room sending orders to another, unknown Commander Ebb.

Commander Ebb took one stride across the room and jerked open the door. The routine ordering of rooms mocked his idea. Commander Ebb felt foolish and a little absurd. He turned back into the little chamber with something like a sigh. Now he saw the book opened at a different page and this time when he picked it up, he read:

Read Me

The remaining pages taunted him with their blankness. Commander Ebb turned to the bookcases: a Bible, some novels, encyclopaedias.

Read Me they all pleaded. But this meant nothing. Nineteenth Century classics in their fine leather and gold bindings remained silent.

Hastily Commander Ebb crossed the hidden chamber and raced across the familiar rooms, up the compelling staircase to the first floor. He threw open the doors to the great library. It had been cleared of books.

In a kind of frantic determination, he felt along its bookcases. Finally, on the highest shelf, Commander Ebb found a folder lying flat and abandoned. Commander Ebb he slid it out and impatiently flipped through its contents with increasing irritation. A small newspaper cutting dated a month previously fell out of the pile. The article about Salt Marsh House was already faded and difficult to read.

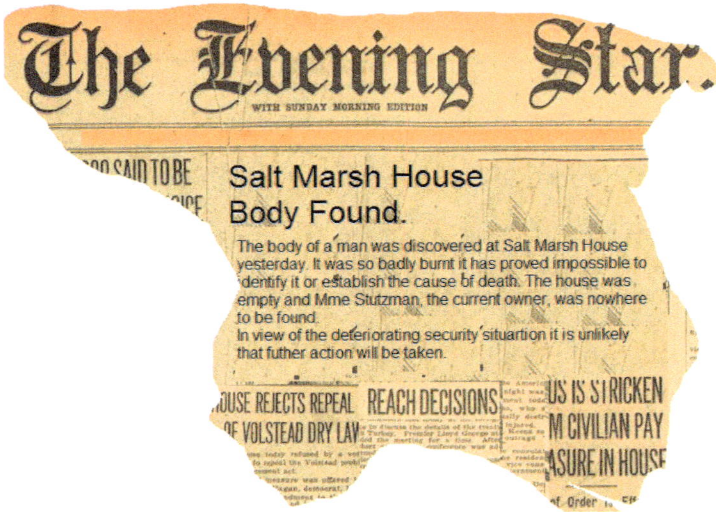

The Evening Star.

WITH SUNDAY MORNING EDITION

Salt Marsh House Body Found.

The body of a man was discovered at Salt Marsh House yesterday. It was so badly burnt it has proved impossible to identify it or establish the cause of death. The house was empty and Mme Stutzman, the current owner, was nowhere to be found.

In view of the deteriorating security situartion it is unlikely that futher action will be taken.

OUSE REJECTS REPEAL OF VOLSTEAD DRY LAW

REACH DECISIONS

US IS STRICKEN M CIVILIAN PAY ASURE IN HOUSE

Commander Ebb went down the stairs with the slim folder under his arm. He shouted for the Private who arrived with ill grace.

'Get me the editor of this paper NOW! Bring him here.' The Private was shaken out of his sullenness. 'Sir?'

'There is a mystery here Private. I will find it out. Don't come back without him, do you hear me?'

'Sir,' said the Private, 'the man is gone. The paper shut down when we arrived. We set up our own paper and people.'

'Then find this journalist,' demanded Commander Ebb. 'Get him here.' The Private went pale as he read the account. 'I'll find him Sir.' He set off raging, he would find him alright.

'You have ONE HOUR,' said Commander Ebb shouting after him. 'One Hour!' He had caught the Private's rage but couldn't quite understand it or its source. He sensed, despite the bright day, a growing awareness of darkness, of ending and not beginning again.

Commander Ebb took a breath and shook off his unaccustomed sense of unease. He returned to the once secret room. He shook open the little file and glanced at the first paper

. **WOMEN'S STATUS IN THE 18TH CENTURY:**

Someone had highlighted the chapter headings.

The unwritten histories of women.

1.	Childbirth	Page 15
2.	Poverty	Page 139
3.	Inheritance	Page 234
4.	Property	Page 345

Commander Ebb wondered at this waste of effort. It was simple. Women did what they always did. Women did what they were told. They cooked, they cleaned, they kept house and they had babies that you made sure were yours. If they died in the endeavour, they died. It was the law. He saw to it. His mother also died under the law. They took their secrets with them.

Men continued to keep the world turning.

Commander Ebb returned to the notebook, but the thought of his mother did not go away. He had returned to his home to find it full of silent relatives. 'She is dead,' his father had said, 'and her baby also.' His father's eyes glowed in his head.

His mother was buried in the town's churchyard and neither Commander Ebb nor any member of his family went again. So young he had been then, but he looked back on himself without compassion. The world had moved on and he with it; he now made the world go around. Sometimes, he felt, he commanded it and this was sweet.

Commander Ebb did not regard the past with any desire. Lost battles, not many, taught him lessons. He learnt to win and planned the future. In general, Commander Ebb believed, life was not as complicated as people said. It could be planned; it could be made more efficient. He would effectively solve this puzzle. He had no doubt.

He turned back to the bookcases in the secret room and noticed for the first time a small, badly bound notebook tucked alongside its more handsome neighbours. It looked as though it had been put together by an amateur. It opened to reveal some handwritten notes; some recipes, some gardening notes, herbal remedies and then at last the same spiky hand that he had seen earlier.

'He is dead and now I am completely alone,' said the writer, *'and so I am writing to you, the future, which I hope one day to see.'*

Noon

.- -. .-

The Private re-entered the house with a curse. He had found the unhappy journalist and rounded him up along with his file of documents.

This time Commander Ebb was too late to prevent him from finding the hidden room. The Journalist following on the Private's heels and gave a slow sigh when he saw it. The Private turned on him.

'Lucky I found him in time Sir, he was about to leave.' The Private hauled the man before his Commander. The Journalist was sweating despite the house's coolness. The Private had made him walk the last mile to the house, driving him on through the blistering noonday sun. In his panic, he had dropped some of his papers but the Private refused to let him pick them up. The documents lay belly up in the road, unmoved by any breath of air. 'No time,' said the Private as he forced the Journalist on.

The Private had left an army vehicle off road a mile from the house and out of view. He told the Journalist it had no fuel but the Journalist knew he was lying. The Private needed the vehicle with sufficient fuel for later. The Journalist knew this too and sweated further in the final march to Salt Marsh House. Commander Ebb looked at his visitor with distaste. The Journalist oozed sweat from every pore. The Private was ordered out. He left, glad of the time to further his own plans.

The little notebook lay open between the two men. Commander Ebb closed its cover. 'Tell me,' he said, 'of the history of this house. Tell me and tell me quickly.' He sat down and stared at the journalist and summed him up: a poor man, unfit, no fighter.

The Journalist shifted on his feet. He was a local and popular. He had the true journalist's skill of being a good listener and people told him their stories. Many of them too dull, common or insignificant to print and he stored them as flotsam and jetsam. But occasionally a story's thread would snag and once he picked it up it would pull him into a maze, unravelling the more he tugged on it. The helpers, the Journalist noticed, were the ones who suffered most. They were abandoned, like Ariadne, on dangerous shores. He himself, in this case, had done his best to aid: to patch the story and stop it tearing further into the fabric of his fragile town. He could see though that Commander Ebb knew nothing of these things; the impossibility of explaining this world.

He licked his lips, started, stuttered and started again.

'The great salt marsh once occupied most of the land closest to the sea. It was known locally as the White Marsh; mainly, it was thought, for the deep fogs that fell on it more frequently than the outlying hills. From their dark heights, you could look over the marshland and see nothing but boiling clouds, seething like milk under the sky.

'But some thought the marsh was named after the White Lady who is rumoured to inhabit its reed beds and a mysterious island in the centre of the marsh. Her appearance changed depending on who saw her.

To some she was a hag, others recounted her loveliness. That she waxed and waned with the moon was a common belief. She existed before the long eternity of the world said others and one who saw her in beauty spent the last of his days searching for her.

He was lost in the White Marsh and never found a safe path home again. Some say he walks there still calling for her, his White Lady. Yet more say she has another terrifying figure; an old, one-eyed creature, hunting, it is said, for children to devour.

'In whatever form she chooses to appear, her appearance always brings misfortune.'

Commander Ebb interrupted abruptly, 'These are fairy tales. Give me facts man! Who lived here and how?'

The Journalist looked at his interrogator and shifted his story.

'For centuries, the townspeople had lived off the marsh, using its reeds and fish for shelter and food. Latterly, though, parts of the marsh were drained for agricultural land. Archaeologists moved in for a while excited by a wood-henge found preserved in the peat with implements from an ancient civilisation. The Mere Hag, an archaeologist postulated, had a historical source; she was a remnant of an old, lost religion, once feared by Christianity.

'The marsh started to retreat and with it the

superstition. Few now feared meeting the Mere Hag when wandering through the reeds and muddy by-ways. The new world proved far more threatening and brought its own myths.'

The Journalist stopped. He worried that he had said too much, but Commander Ebb waved him on with a flick of his hand.

'Salt Marsh House once stood near the centre of the marsh, some miles from its neighbours. But much of the marsh was drained and developed, so now it stands on fine agricultural land at the edge of town. The house had been built by those who believed in the White Lady. Over the years, various builders uncovered small charms or animals built into the fabric of the walls. Magic spells were carved across portals and inglenooks, in fact any entrance where air, and therefore the Mere Hag, could enter the building.'

The Journalist fumbled in his pockets and

produced a small photo.

'You see the full moon and scratched *M?* It's from the fireplace in the library.'

Commander Ebb shrugged his indifference and so the Journalist continued.

'About this time, my research shows, the White Lady also began to be seen as the Queen of the Dead seeking justice for any that were wronged in their lifetime.'

Commander Ebb slapped his hand down on the book in front of him. 'I have no interest in this,' he said impatiently. 'This is not the real world!'

The unfortunate Journalist resumed his

story.

'The mid-seventeen hundreds saw the house fall into poverty. The local squire had gambled his wealth away and the estate was mortgaged twice over. Bad weather and subsequent poor harvests had further weakened the family and at last when the squire died, his son, William Goldi, found he had inherited only debt and a tumble-down property.

'William shut the house up and went to the capital to make his fortune. He returned a year later with a wealthy fiancée—a widow, Elizabeth, who was at least twice his age. The marriage caused a sensation in the town and it was rumoured that William's sister begged him on her knees not to marry a woman who surely could not provide him with heirs.

'But the wedding went ahead anyway and is still talked of now. No luxury was spared and contemporary reports of its extravagance and an oil painting of the happy couple forms a central part of the town's local museum, although how the museum fares these days, I could not say.

'One newspaper report of the day commented on the beauty of the bride's dress without extending the compliment to the bride herself. An instance of journalistic spite, I noted, but have never seen it picked up by any other commentator.

'William Goldi lost no time in spending his wife's money on refurbishing Salt Marsh House. He added its elegant exterior and repaired the fine library, wine cellars and extensive grounds. 'Once he had his hands on her wealth, William did not spare his wife. He condemned Elizabeth for her inability to bear children and during the regular parties he held for the county, he ignored his wife completely or scolded her so ferociously she would leave. Gradually and then generally, Elizabeth withdrew from social gatherings so she was barely looked for or expected at them. Her young husband indulged himself and several sons of the town were thought to be his and expected much from their father whilst he was alive and more when he was dead.'

The Journalist paused as Commander Ebb began to jot down details in the diary's margins. The nib of his pen scratched out erratic sounds across the page. The Commander glanced up to clarify his notes, 'The Goldis lived here in the 18th Century?' he asked.

He is not used to writing, observed the Journalist with some astonishment. Commander Ebb's strong hand was clenched uncomfortably about his pen. The Journalist confirmed the dates and continued.

'Imagine then the surprise of the town and

family when, on a rare appearance, his wife appeared, clearly pregnant. In due course, she gave birth to a healthy boy who was christened Corvin. A harsh sound for so small a boy...'

Commander Ebb wrote down *Corvin [Goldie?] – child of Elizabeth Goldie.* He attached the names to each other using a dotted line.

He takes things very literally thought the Journalist watching him, before picking up his thread again.

'Elizabeth died of fever within days. William Goldi found himself with an heir he had to acknowledge because of his wife's seclusion, but believed in his heart could not be his. He buried Elizabeth privately and commissioned a tomb of black marble. A black angel held a black baby and hung over the last line of our Lord's Prayer:

DELIVER US FROM EVIL

'It was placed in the darkest corner of the church and is there now, entirely unremarked. Elizabeth had no close family to mourn her and her little son's future lay entirely in the hands of William Goldi.'

'He should have beaten it out of her,' said Commander Ebb suddenly, 'It's weakness otherwise.'

The journalist, interrupted, suddenly found himself unable to continue. Commander Ebb rose to his feet. 'We will stop for a moment but you will remain in the house.'

He called for the Private who came after a short delay. 'Show the man to a room. Give him refreshments. Give him half an hour and then return him here.' But it was not the journalist who needed the break.

Commander Ebb paced around the room and rigorously forced himself to wait for five minutes. He looked out at the bright day through the window. He saw the sun had reached its zenith; already, at the edges of the sky, he saw night was preparing to draw in.

Unconsciously, his fingers drummed an irregular beat on the table.

.... --- -. --- ..- .-.

He drew the notebook to him and started to read again.

He is dead and I am alone. So, I am writing to you the future that I hope one day to see.

I came as a young girl to Salt Marsh House, the unfortunate Ana Goldi, no more than seven years old. Who my mother is or was remains a mystery to me. I was not the first child to be left at Salt Marsh House and I was not the last, but I was the only one who survived.

As he read, Commander Ebb became aware of a lost memory rising from the pages, hands held out towards him. His heart beat faster, but the thing had gone, slipping as quickly out of his mind as it had entered.

Commander Ebb leafed through the notebook; there was nothing else to be read although the last section contained faint grey writing that seemed to him to be fading with the sun.

.- -. .-

Unexpectedly he smelt a familiar perfume, a shimmer of something and then—a hook turned in his stomach. Blood filled him. He stumbled through the door of the main hall, ran out of the house and on into the grounds where he spewed up. Choking, he straightened, and looked out over the marsh's horizon. He could taste salt in his mouth. Then he heard the landscape screaming. Out of the darkness caused by taste and pain, a high-pitched wailing seemed to crawl towards him.

The war was lost, he remembered, his last successful battle counted for nothing. He recalled his night-marches and his command, merciless in the darkness; the cries that then had left him unmoved.

Commander Ebb stared into the salt marshes and could not decide if the sobbing he heard was his own. He reached into his jacket, pulled out a flask and drank from it. Looking back at the house he saw a white figure gazing down from a first-floor window. He made his way towards it, stumbling across the garden's paths.

The Private met him at the door with a crooked smile. 'Journalist's gone Sir,' the Private informed him, 'ran out toward the marsh while my back was turned getting fuel for a fire.'

This was true at least, Commander Ebb thought, the Private reeked of petrol and burning. 'Not sure he'll get through,' the Private continued, 'full of phantoms and flickering lights.'

A rage seized Commander Ebb. 'You've failed!' He said. He seized the Private by the throat, choking him before punching him to the ground. Finally, Commander Ebb kicked him in the throat. His booted foot landed solidly on the man's exposed neck.

'Don't you *ever* fail me again,' he said before stepping over the fallen Private to return to Salt Marsh House.

Afternoon

.- -. .-

The sun was falling out of the sky and trees cast great green shadows across Salt Marsh House by the time the Bagman returned.

He entered through the great door and walked across the hall before he had a sense of being watched. Someone was looking down at him from the great gallery. Out of the corner of his eye he saw a frail figure walk away into the upper hall. The Bagman raced up the stairs and along the corridor, but whoever it was had gone. The Bagman opened countless doors onto vacant rooms before coming into the bookless library.

'And rich men look as pale as their white money.' The phrase ran through the Bagman's mind as clearly as if it had been said aloud; as if somebody had leaned in from the otherworld and breathed it in his living ear. Across the library, the Bagman clearly saw Commander Ebb's drained face hanging outside the window, staring in with livid

eyes.

Before the Bagman could cry out, Commander Ebb moved from the frame's shadow, his reflection stirring and dissolving in the window where he had been gazing out over the marsh. 'Did you see her Bagman?' he said without looking up, without seeming even to see him entering the room.

'Saw something Sir,' said the Bagman with a shudder. He was not a man for mystery. 'But it's gone now.' He surveyed the room anxiously and his fingers explored a length of empty shelving behind his back, out of sight of Commander Ebb. Then the Bagman's face brightened. The house had kept his secret at least. A small wad of notes that he had stored earlier was still there.

He moved out toward the centre of the room.

As though partnering him in a dance

Commander Ebb turned to face him and deliberately stepped towards him. 'I keep finding writing,' he told the Bagman. 'Everywhere I go I find fragments of writing.'

The Bagman was confused. 'There is nothing here Sir, no papers.' He spoke slowly as if to a child or a frightened girl. 'Who could be writing? There is no-one but us.'

Commander Ebb reached out and put his hand on the Bagman's shoulder; he spun him round. 'Don't you see man,' he said urgently—'don't you see it!'

The Bagman scanned the empty shelves and a few books that had fallen to the floor. The spines and their bindings were resolutely shut, but he felt the concentration of the man behind him. The Bagman examined the room again—he could not see what Commander Ebb was referring to. 'There is no …' he began and then he stopped. For he saw it too and felt the shock.

In the centre of the room in the middle of the dusty, untrodden floor was the single word

Ana

Beside it was the tiny handprint of a child.

Commander Ebb smiled bleakly at the Bagman and bowed as if at the end of a stately dance. Then he turned and made his way through the silent house, the Bagman following him.

Commander Ebb returned to the hidden chamber. The Bagman started at the sight of it. The room gleamed as though untouched by any external influence. Once again, its surfaces were free from dust. The Bagman took in its atmosphere with one piercing glance. He doubted the Private had maintained its pristine properties and in the cool air he could distinctly smell … 'Perfume,' said Commander Ebb, studying him as though the

Bagman was a test, a singing canary in a cage.

The Bagman met his eyes and held his gaze. 'There's no cheap women been here,' he said thoughtfully, 'no piece of stuff for the Private to play with.'

'Nor you, I suppose?' said Commander Ebb moving towards him, his mouth close to the Bagman's ear. 'No Sir,' said the Bagman. He was a family man at heart. The countless small deals, he told himself, were always for them.

Subconsciously he tapped a seam of his bag. With a sigh, Commander Ebb turned away back to the desk. He sat down and re-opened the notebook.

'Leave me now, 'he told the Bagman quietly. 'Leave me!' The final sentence was a whisper but the Bagman obeyed as if it had been a shout. Instantly and with fear.

Commander Ebb turned the page and found as he knew he would, a crumbling text in brown gold ink that sank through the brittle leaves of the book. Each entry like a ghost containing the mirror imprints of text from the other side.

June 14th 1782

Salt Marsh House

Page one.

I am Ana Goldi, Mistress of Salt Marsh House and I am writing to you, the future, that I hope one day to see.

When I first came here, I was a child. One summer's day found me waiting under a turquoise sky. It's the first morning I remember clearly, the first day of my life. The morning planet still held her place in the sky.

I was so scared. I remember that fear burrowed into me. An old man took me to the house, not speaking a word, neither on the journey nor at the door where he left me.

Terror filled me and, when the black door was opened, overwhelmed me. I could not move to cross the threshold. The maid expressed no surprise at my presence. She tutted at my immobility. She thrust out her bony arm and pulled me into the house.

'The Star sent you,' she said to us, 'you belong to us now.'

I remember staring about in bewildered horror. In crossing the threshold my memories vanished. I wanted to leave but didn't know how. I knew only one thing with clarity. No star had brought me; I was a human child and had come from the earth and warmth. I can see myself now, cold and frightened, struggling to breathe in the sharp, bright hall of Salt Marsh House.

'You wait,' said the maid. 'You wait there.' She left briefly and then returned with some clothes, a petticoat, a wool shift dress, a long waistcoat, a belt and small shoes. She made me strip naked and change in the hall, and then took my old clothes out to be burnt.

While she was away, I looked up the great stairs; there I saw a young boy of about fourteen. He was darkly handsome and already as sharp as steel. He smiled slowly when he saw me looking at him. 'I saw you,' he said, 'I saw everything.' He ran lightly down the stairs to where I stood and approached as if to kiss me, but instead he bit me on the lips. 'I am Corvin Goldi,' he told me, 'you belong to me now. Everything belongs to me now, or will do.' Then he walked out of the great door and was gone.

Trembling, I gazed around me. The vast and sinister staircase climbed and wound round the walls like a serpent. Its dark, rich steps gleaming as so many scales. Under my breath, I counted each stair until my gaze reached the galleried first floor landing and a sudden commotion shattered the silence. A woman opened a door and called loudly for help. Then I saw her, her dress shimmering against the lustrous wood of the curved balustrades. Impatiently, the woman called again and then glanced down. I saw her pale face hanging above me. She observed me coolly and then clapped her hands in sharp command. 'Child, what are you doing there!' she exclaimed. 'I need your eyes. Come! Bring them up here.'

I do not know how long it took to reach her. Moments only no doubt, but then I felt I was toiling up a monster's back and took me days. I walked up, as if to a scaffold. Sometimes, I think, I walk them still.

As I climbed, I noticed at my leisure, some dried flowers and tiny unremarked pins that had fallen from dresses or buttonholes and now lodged in the stair's intricate turnings.

Once I gained the first floor, I was hustled into a beautiful room. A piece of embroidery was stretched over a frame that stood before the fireplace. All was flooded by light from the windows and with a vision sharpened by fear, I studied the scene covering the simple piece of linen; a little bear had been stitched into life. Each detail of its fur and the grasses it sat on had been drawn out in silk. The beast gleamed under the silver light of an embroidered moon.

The woman pinched me to make me look up. Then she picked out a sharp, fine needle from the frame and cut a length from a skein of silk. 'Thread this,' she instructed, 'for I cannot!' I took the items to the window and pausing my breath so my body would not move, slipped the thread home through the pierced and piercing steel.

This simple thing sealed my fate.

The woman who worked such beautiful items intervened with her brother, the Master of Salt Marsh House—William Goldi. This time, she was more successful. This time, he listened to her. 'Sister,' he said, 'Mrs. Towlinson—if you think the girl quick and useful, I will keep her.' So it was, I became companion to his widowed Sister and she would teach me all her skills in needlework.

But I knew this gradually only later. I felt only the anger of the maid when she saw me with Mrs. Towlinson and her realisation that my role had changed. The maid showed me quickly to an old room at the top of the house, a skylight revealed tall chimneys above me. The room held only a single bed, a pot and a pitcher of water. The maid left me a small meal, told me she would fetch me in the morning and went out locking the door behind her. I heard her footsteps walking down the corridor and then in the silence knew I was alone in the east wing of Salt Marsh House.

The moon rose over the chimneys and glowed

---

into my room. Eventually I pulled the bed under the skylight and climbed on it to open the old window. But when I peered out over the expectant and breathing marsh I was seized with a horror that was colder than the night air.

In the black shadow of the reeds, I saw the Mere Hag step out and walk unswervingly towards the house that seemed even now to be falling into the marsh.

The next morning the maid found me shocked in my bed but she showed no sympathy when I told her what I had seen. 'You are mad,' was all she said. Then, forcing me to dress, she showed me downstairs to the great hall. The windows were thrown open and on mahogany sideboards, flowers in crystal vases scented the air and their colourful reflections fell across marbled floors.

Afternoon

June 14th 1782 Salt Marsh House Ana Goldi

Mrs. Towlinson waited for me, gazing out across the marsh. She wore, I remember, a day dress embroidered with silver reeds and golden flowers. The housekeeper was with her, whispering. She glanced at me when I came in and the conversation ceased. Mrs. Towlinson turned from the window and walked towards me. I sensed already she half regretted her impulse of the day before.

'She may do,' she said doubtfully. Then, to the housekeeper— 'If she is to be a useful companion, she will need to read. She will share lessons with Corvin Goldi, our little prince of Salt Marsh House, my charming nephew.' Her lips twitched when she said Corvin's name and I felt a contained anger within her. Mrs. Towlinson turned me over to the housekeeper without another word.

Commander Ebb stopped reading with a sigh;

Afternoon

June 14th 1782 Salt Marsh House Ana Goldi

the pages were again completely blank. A door suddenly opened in his own mind and there he saw his mother: she was resting in an old arm chair. She was golden in the sunlight that filtered through the window as she sat nursing her baby. When Commander Ebb entered the room, she looked up and smiled. But he did not smile back and so she had gazed at him, doubt showing in her face.

Commander Ebb turned his back on the unbidden memory. *Why think of that now?* He returned to the diary and opened it at random. He found another page of faded ink.

Ana Goldi continued her history.

Afternoon

June 14th 1782 Salt Marsh House Ana Goldi

June 14th 1782

Salt Marsh House

Page two.

I liked to read and read widely, but for all his riches, Corvin Goldi could not follow me. Rigid in his certainties, language taught him little. He was given one limited and life long sentence of his own - '*You are entitled.*' Once he had learnt that, he learnt nothing else.

I loved needlework above reading and spent more time sewing than between the pages of a book. With my needle and thread, I wove cloths and embroidered gowns of great beauty. Soon they were worn and displayed throughout the great house and much admired. Mrs. Towlinson gave one of her rare smiles when she heard me praised and kept me by her.

I read to her in the long evenings and often her brother, William Goldi, would join us.

Salt Marsh House ran to the rhythms of the seasons and was nightly shut up against thieves and the Mere Hag. In this, William Goldi was diligent. He feared her more than breaking and assaults against his property. But she visited all the same. Regularly when the moon was waning, I would spy her from the skylight, moving towards us, casting long shadows before her, she never stopping at any of the doorways or pausing at the inscriptions that were meant to keep her out.

The housekeeper and the maids looked askance if I mentioned seeing her or the sound of crying children that I often heard at her visits. I soon learnt not to speak of her again.

Looking back now, I see figures that spoke and

yet did not tell. I have searched and read through the books and the texts and all the dusty writings on forgotten shelves, looking and looking for some explanation of why I was and how I had come here.

At this a thin bitter smile twisted the face of Commander Ebb. 'I would sympathize more,' he said, 'If I were not in the same house, repeating the same.' Commander Ebb jumped. He had spoken out loud and the Private, who had silently entered the room, was watching him with an expression of detailed malice.

Afternoon

June 14th 1782 Salt Marsh House Ana Goldi

Evening

.– –. .–

The Private handed some sheets of paper to Commander Ebb, 'Found these on the road, Sir.' The slight emphasis on the last word did not give his tone respect. 'The Journalist, the fool, dropped them.'

Commander Ebb looked at the livid bruises on the Private's neck with a shudder. 'You disgust me,' he said, 'Why are you still here?' The Private returned his Commander's gaze. 'Can't get rid of me *Sir* I belong with you – besides where else is there to go?'

It was a statement of fact. By now even the lowliest soldier knew what defeat was. The mountains encircling the plain had cut off all line of retreat. Ahead of them lay the White Marsh and the sea. Fragmented and disjointed, the army was beginning to fall apart; each man dealing with unaccustomed failure in his own way, trying to make a future in which they could live.

Evening

The Private sat down on the carpet, his back against the wall and lolled his head against the painted plaster, watching his Commander. The Private lit a cigarette and blew the smoke upwards, struck another match and contemplated the flame. 'Such a thing of beauty,' he said. 'Such power in a tiny splinter of wood. Makes me happy each time I see it. Gives me *life* every time I feel it.' He sprang unexpectedly to his feet. 'Let me show you what it can do. Let me show you what you *should* do with found letters written by strangers!' He dropped a second lighted match on the edge of the papers he had handed to Commander Ebb. The papers caught and started to curl rapidly in the heat, smoke smudging the air.

Swiftly Commander Ebb pounced his hand upon the pages, beating out the delicate heat, saving the fragile text. 'You'll regret that,' said the Private, and laughing he left the room.

The smouldering papers before Commander Ebb were a collection of handwritten notes and magazine articles. An interview with Salt Marsh House's new owners, Commander Ebb noted, was produced shortly before his army had taken the town. He studied the picture of Mme Stutzman and realised he must have missed her by only a few days.

Illustrated Life - Society News

Illustrated Life welcomes new arrivals the Stutzmans to our town. Famous interior decorator Romain Stutzman was invalided out of the army last year and has bought Salt Marsh House.

He plans an ambitious project of works to restore its historic features. 'I lost my leg, not my eyes or my fortune thank God!' Mr. Stutzman jokes. 'And together with my wife, I am looking forward to researching the history of the house and investing in its restoration.'

Mme Ana Stutzman—pictured—a well known horticulturalist is also interested in the early design of its grounds. Mme Stutzman tells IL magazine, 'it's so exciting to research this original layout.'

Both were amused when they were asked if they had heard of the ghosts that were said to inhabit the house. 'We do not fear the dead,' says Romain. 'And anyway,' adds Mme Stutzman, 'a beautiful garden will always restore lost souls. We plan to make this a place of peace now and after the war.'

On that positive note the interview ended.

(Salt Marsh House will feature in our Decorators and Home Supplement—Autumn Edition).

The Stutzmans were unfortunate to choose that region to see out the war Commander Ebb thought. His unit had dispensed rough justice to keep the town in some kind of order. The people loathed each other, he had noted, as much as the invading forces.

She is beautiful though, he thought, studying the charred photo and Commander Ebb breathed in again a perfume from the room. He gazed at the snapshot, as if he had never seen a woman before.

There were no further articles from Illustrated Life and there was no evidence Mme Stutzman had made any start on her gardening plans. The lawns stretched without respite to their wooded boundaries and the old beds and borders were filled with gnarled roses and weeds.

Commander Ebb picked out a newspaper article and continued to read. He gave a dark smile as he read about the war he was fighting.

The Evening Star.

...O SAID TO BE ...SON'S CHOICE ...R PRESIDENCY

Sectarian violence spreads: mass grave found.

A harrowing sectarian war has spread across the region this month and a mass grave has been found on the edge of White Marsh to the south of the town.

"It's so sad we have reached this point," said a local priest. "The violences seems to have gathered a relentless momentum that has defied the attempts of both sides of the residents to stanch it.

The priest blamed local government officals for fermenting tensions even while preparing for war. The priest added, " I feel, disgusted at what's happening here' and I am afraid of what might happen next."

TURKIS... FALL...

...WINTER'S HARDEST STORM HITS WEST

INTERNATIONAL... FOR GERM...

NEW JERSEY SE...

Really, thought Commander Ebb, killing was not as complicated or strange as the priest made out. God had very little to do with it. Commander Ebb observed that people killed each other simply and without much need of a state to encourage them. In his mind he summarized:

1. Naked self-interest—public or private
2. Transgression from Honour –

A welcome remembered line ran through his mind...*'I could not love thee Dear, so much...'*

These poems and their heroic couplets had informed his childhood reading and built a man. Unconsciously they had become the rhythm of his body; they had patterned and cut out his mind to their beats. He remembered reciting them to his beloved father who had lit up at the sight of his small boy reciting the lines with such fervour. 'You see my son,' he said. 'Honour is everything. When you grow up, you will be responsible for the honour of your house and your family.'

Commander Ebb's mother had walked into the room at this point and kissed him. 'We count on you,' his father told him and swept him up into an exuberant embrace.

'...Loved I not honour more.' The poem

concluded.

And I myself, thought Commander Ebb, *am an honourable man.*

A second newspaper clipping caught his attention and roused him with a start.

With regret this paper announces the death of Mr. Romain Stutzman who was killed in

Who looked after her then? thought Commander Ebb, *she was too beautiful to live long alone.* For the first time he considered with concern an unknown victim's fate.

Commander Ebb stood up and examined

the tapestries in the room. He wondered if these were the ones Ana Goldi had worked on; if so, that must be over two hundred years ago. Two hundred years from now, he asked himself, who would think of me; he who had never written a word other than an instructed order.

For the first time, he thought, *Who Am I?* and not *Who Are You?*

He could not leave, he realised, until he found out.

Startled by a fragrance, Commander Ebb looked around the beautiful chamber but it remained empty. The perfume is in the diary, he told himself, with its secrets. It is nothing.

He remembered walking through a similar room, a letter in his hand. His mother when she saw him looked up and smiled. The smile dying on her lips as she gazed at her son and saw his face in the sun-lit house.

Commander Ebb thrust the memory out of his mind. It was for the best, he told himself and he knew it. He turned over a page and a small fragment of poetry fluttered out.

To The White Lady – Time's Stitch

When I do count the lost and lonely dead
And read they lie not quietly down the days
As they, cast off by snapping, fragile thread
Spy broken kin plot open shallow graves.
Then do the lie stirred dead stand, bolt upright
To prick out ghosts of Truth, water our fears
And graft old wrongs in garden's inky night.
Still borne, yet breathing in our new-found ears
They cry aloud in present Justice' halls.
We, living now, must count the cost of gain
Our worm rich houses wound with biting gall,
Dyeing old yarns, while love is worked in vain.
Folded and quartered, penned in I alone,
In Truth's sharp eye, Right writes to hem me home.

AN-Anon

Commander Ebb scanned the poem and tore the thing up. An anonymous author was of no use to him. Abstracts were of no use to him. This was not what he was looking for. He reached again for the paper but a different hand met him on the page: he had found the diaries of Ana Stutzman, the current owner of Salt Marsh House.

.– –. .–

Salt Marsh House
19TH May - page one.

He is dead, my husband, my Romain. My husband Romain is dead.

Butchered in our home town by people we took for friends. Our friends who came to our house and ate at our table. We talked of gardens and planting. Of art and literature. We gave gifts and laughed. When our friends were sick we visited, when we were ill, they called. We cared for their children as we had none of our own. We were guardians to babies whose parents cut us to pieces.

We were outsiders and always outcast. But we did not know that then. When the war came here, all changed. There were so many outcasts that the town queued to kill them. They dug a narrow trench but it was too small to layer the dead. In the panic, the dead were buried upright, shoulder to shoulder and living friends stamped the earth down over heads and *up-flung hands.*

After his murder one of Romain's colleagues came to me. In my grief, I thought his visit out of kindness for my lost husband. But I mistook him. For he took me and afterwards said 'you belong to me now, everything belongs to me now.' Then he walked out of the great door of this, my husband's house, our house, my house and was gone.

Each night he returned until once, when he lay smiling, I killed him and dragged his body to the lawns and burnt it. So much petrol, the grasses blazed with him. I have found a hidden room and I stay there. They are dead and now I am alone and so I am writing to you, my little book and the future I hope one day to see.

•– –• •– •••

Evening

Salt Marsh House, 19th May – Ana Stutzman diary

With a start, Commander Ebb rose to his feet. *She is still here,* he thought.

In a mirrored room—his mother stood to meet him, the child in her arms, her face as white as the card in his hand. He did not see her. He could not see her.

He would see *her.* Ana Stutzman, he would find her, he would save her, and together they would begin again and replace lost children.

'She Is Still Here!'

Commander Ebb yelled the words out loud, the noise startling in the closed chamber. Yet no other breath stirred in the cool air or eyes fixed on his. Only the Private opened the door and joined him. The bruises around his neck were extending to meet his half closed and blackened eye.

'Of course *she* is still here, *Sir,*' he said coolly. 'How do you think they can leave when they are part of your bones? However hard you try to shut them up in small rooms and keep them quiet, covering them with cloths! Burying them in graves will not quieten them. Where can they go without taking you with them? Where you are, *she* is also.'

'Take care man,' said Commander Ebb, 'or I will close your mouth along with your eye. If you know her, bring her here. You have one hour.'

The Private gave a salute that was both mocking and exhausted. 'In half that time, Sir,' he said. 'Or nothing. The day is ending.'

He left, leaving the door open and through it, Commander Ebb could see the Bagman who was whistling as he opened cupboards in search of food and stowing his small tins of money. The Bagman looked up unabashed as the Commander joined him. 'I take what I find Sir,' he explained. 'Small things to carry back to my home. Will need to get back soon Sir,' he said, 'it will be too dangerous to stay here much longer—for us.'

The Bagman paused in his packing. He is effective, thought Commander Ebb; the Bagman had plucked quantities of jewellery from lost houses. If he lived, he would be rich. The Bagman looked at him. 'Come with me Sir,' he urged, 'I know a way back through the mountains. We have behaved as heroes.' The Bagman repeated his Commander's previous speeches, 'we have behaved as men should. History will not forget us. We will go home, heads high—with honour.'

The Bagman beckoned him to follow as he made his way out through a side entrance of the house.

Commander Ebb turned back to look at Salt Marsh House. The setting sun was turning the lawns and trees red and black. The house darkened against branches that seemed, to Commander Ebb, to press down low on the horizon.

The man is right. I must go now, he thought. He gripped the Bagman's shoulder. 'Wait for me.' he entreated, 'an hour only.' But the Bagman refused. 'We need to go now Sir. Look!' He pointed at the plains. They could clearly see silhouettes of lines of men making their steady way towards them.

The Bagman continued. 'There is one path through the marsh that eventually cuts towards the mountains. That is the path to take Sir. But we need to go now. We have guns, food and money. I carry nothing else, we need nothing else.' The man was pleading. 'Sir—Please as I love you, leave now with me. Nothing waits for you here.'

But looking back, Commander Ebb saw the Private watching him. And as if compelled he released the Bagman and began to walk back to Salt Marsh House.

The Bagman clutched his arm again and spun Commander Ebb round to face the marsh. 'Everyone who has fled the house took a path through the marsh. It is an old route known by traffickers. They took people, children and goods this way—time out of mind. We can get through to the mountains and then home.' The Bagman squatted down and squinted through the reeds. From that level it was possible to discern a faint track that seemed to curve down towards the sea. The grasses were bronze against the soft earth. Small birds crept between the reeds - their feathers were gilded by the setting sun.

'It's tidal,' the Bagman observed, 'and we can only move when it's turning, when it ebbs out.' He stood up and faced his Commander once more. Looking at his face, the Bagman clearly read he was arguing a lost cause. With a shrug, he picked up his rucksack and made off. When he reached the beginning of the path through the marshes, he looked back.

The Commander had not moved. The Bagman pulled out a coin that flashed golden in the sunset. The Commander noted it dully. He saw the Bagman put the coin down as a tiny marker for him to follow and then return to his path. Commander Ebb could see the movement of reeds for some distance and then—nothing.

Commander Ebb took one step to follow the Bagman, but the Private had seen him from the House and joined him. Commander Ebb regarded the Private's livid face. 'There is a body, Sir,' the Private informed him, 'been covered up—best come back Sir, if I were you.' They turned and walked back to the house, the Private lagging behind, shadowing the Commander's footsteps, both returning inevitably to the hidden room.

It remained as Commander Ebb had left it.

He turned to face the Private. 'There is nothing new here. Nothing to see.' Commander Ebb turned on the man, who faced him down, staring out at him through swollen eyelids. 'And yet *Sir*, I see it clearly. It astonishes me you can't. That you are so sightless—for all your reading.'

The Private raised his swollen hand, to touch his swollen neck. Then he smiled suddenly, a smile so bright that for a moment Commander Ebb was confused; that he was suddenly transported to another room where people were smiling, where someone was smiling but who it was he could not now remember. The Private handed him a letter. 'Best keep reading Sir, what you are seeking will find you soon enough.'

He felt in his pocket for a cigarette but struggled to light it with his bruised fingers. Finally, Commander Ebb struck a match for him and as the flame took hold, the Private took in a deep sucking breath and drew the cigarette into life. In that moment, Commander Ebb felt that all Time spiralled around him and all was present and all was racing past him and all was lost.

The Private regarded his Commander coldly, noted the thinning hair, a once handsome face declining into age and the beginning of something—something new.

No, not fear, thought the Private, *but something like - an absence perhaps?* He briefly considered, but did not care enough to pin it down. He turned and left the room.

Commander Ebb clutched blindly at the Journalist's letters that lay unread on the table before him. There was no order to the documents so he pulled one out at random. To his surprise, he saw it was a note and formed letters between the journalist and Ana Stutzman. Some predated the war.

The Journalist, Commander Ebb noted, used only a typewriter and he could see carbon stains on some of the paper. Ana, as he knew already, had a rich, curved hand, always in black ink. Many of the letters were charred and incomplete.

To Ana Stutzman from the Journalist

SALT MARSH HOUSE

April 15th

Dear Ana,

Thanks so much for your note and the photo. As you know I have been researching the House's history for some time now and am so grateful you have contacted me.

I can't say I am surprised that you have found a hidden room in Salt Marsh House. I understand a previous chamber was found tucked behind the library about fifty years ago and was incorporated as a study. Surprisingly, I always thought, that room was never properly investigated. It just seemed to be welcomed as unexpected additional space. Certainly there is no record of any found text or documents and why it was sealed up has been a mystery.

Of course I would love to see the room you have uncovered and grateful to see any papers you have found there.

Thanks once more for thinking of me.

Your friend, the Journalist.

Ana Stutzman to the Journalist

C/O The Star Offices

April 19th

Just a quick note to say I enjoyed your write-up in ***Illustrated Life.*** *However, Romain is unhappy that the comment about his fortune was left in.*

He seems to think it may cause a problem locally and bring us unwelcome attention. I think he is over reacting but we need to discuss who has final editorial control over our articles for Decorators and Home edition.

The last thing we want to do is to upset the town when we are trying to make Salt Marsh House a place of sanctuary in these dangerous times.

Can you meet for lunch? I am sure we can sort this out between us and I have finally begun to transcribe some of the writing I found in the hidden room.

The Journalist to Ana Stutzman

SALT MARSH HOUSE
22 April
Dear Ana,

I wasn't sure from our last conversation whether I had understood you properly. Are you saying that you are continuing to find old documents—or are you suggesting that the writing is being renewed each day?

Please clarify. I cannot overstate this matter enough. If we are going to publish a definitive record of the house and garden, we cannot afford to be taken in by any hoax.

In the meantime, I suggest checking the handwriting against archives held in the town. We need to decide whether this has been written by a clerk or an original author. Is there any chance of getting to the great library in Strasbourg? -

They are sure to have an extensive record but know this is not an easy journey these days.

Your Friend, The Journalist.

Romain Stutzman to his wife – Ana Stutzman

To: Ana Stutzman

SALT MARSH HOUSE

25th April

Dearest Ana,

I arrived in Strasbourg safely although, Ana, the cathedral and the surrounding streets have been severely damaged in the latest riots. It breaks my heart to see these beautiful buildings so mistreated.

However, I did manage to track down the cathedral archivist who had luckily moved the entire archive into a place of safety. I have sent a parcel of documents to you under separate post.

I think we can safely say the handwriting is original and passes scientific tests on the ink and paper. We have to look elsewhere than a hoax for our mysterious texts.

page two...

Another odd thing—the documents I have sent you weren't accurately indexed. The archivist thinks they have been deliberately misplaced. The only reason we found them at all was I suddenly glanced away from the cards and saw a piece of paper poking out from a separate file. I was amazed to recognise poor Ana Goldi's handwriting. We weren't sure if these had recently gone astray when the archive was moved or whether her animated accounts have been deliberately buried in the index.

Of course now you will see that they

should have been classified under...

But here the letter ended – a confused smudge of smoke and brittle blackened paper.

Letter from Ana Stutzman to the Journalist

C/O The Star Office
5th May

Sorry not to have replied earlier. I have received the post from Romain and have shut myself up to have time to go through them. I am beginning to get some background to Salt Marsh House and clearly it's much earlier than we had imagined. I am very excited! Romain is fascinated and has written again from Strasbourg.

I am looking forward to his coming home, but I think he may have a point about this region's hostility. I walked into town the other day to help out at the local school. There was such an odd atmosphere when I went into the classroom I didn't stay very long. The women grouped together and just stared. It was very uncomfortable. Of course the children pick up on it.

The city council blames outsiders for the Cathedral's destruction, but Romain strongly suspects local authorities had a hand to play in it. The archivist told him he had to defend the library, not against an angry populace, but from the university scholars themselves.

It's a relief to have a project to work on and Salt Marsh House is just what I need to occupy me and keep me from worrying.

I am beginning to wonder if we

don't have an original Hall House hidden inside our home. It's like everything else; once you know what you are looking for you can see it clearly. But a lost hall would explain many of the unexpected or 'hidden' rooms that turn up from time to time. They are probably nothing more than unplanned spaces, left behind when the house was remodeled.

But that doesn't account for the room I found, with its rich decoration and definite sense of purpose. To me it seems to do two things at once: conceal a story and reveal it.

I am enclosing some of the documents that Romain supplied. You can see the writing matches the fragments we found in the hidden room—and yes, the categorisations are in place.

You are such a stickler for facts my little journalist friend!

Write soon.

Love

Ana.

Enclosed documents catalogued by a local historian.

Document SMH-AG 0001

Copy of notebook entry by Ana Goldi.

SALT MARSH HOUSE 5th May 1782

I am Ana Goldi and I am writing to you - the future - that I hope one day to see.

I am the wife of Salt Marsh House, yet only here, shut up in this room, do I feel secure. While I sit here and write, I look out and see danger walking towards me. I hear false accusation at my keyhole. I feel the House begin to fall into the Marsh. When I am here, I believe the horror cannot cross the threshold and find me. Here, alone of all the rooms in Salt Marsh

House, I will be safe.

If I look through my great books of law, I believe that I will find one little sentence that will protect me from the greater one that is drawing to my door. I write another's sentence – but it is my sentence also.

Had I, my lords, been born crested not cloven you had not treated me thus!

I am cloven all the way through. I am split and I am broken. My body swells with pain, my belly swells with child. I am lawfully placed and yet I threaten the law and its possessions. *'And rich men look as pale as their white money.'* They discuss things gravely and believe I cannot hear.

Enclosed documents catalogued by a local historian.

Document SMH-CG0001

Dated

Salt Marsh House 6th May 1782

Copy of a letter from Corvin Goldi to his friend Johann Carolus

—Owner of Gutenberg Press in Strasbourg

To Gutenberg Press: Strasbourg
Johann Carolus 6th May 1782

Dear Friend,

There is still a problem unresolved in this house—but it grows greater everyday with the belly of my step-mother Ana Goldi

I am writing to you as I know your skill with the textures of our times.

I am the entitled heir to Salt Marsh House yet you know, as well as any man, the doubt with which my father considers me.

I too grow pregnant as I conceive the *idea* of a work against me. Ana has charmed him out of all reason.

What fell day sent her to my house; she should have been rid with the rest of them. I should have seen to it rather than watching her white body. Her nakedness then is nothing to her nakedness now.

My friend—advise me what I should do. I am spitting needles! This marriage and this baby ruin me but I am unable to speak one word to my father.

He will not hear any utterance against her. You know well the potential of my estate and my generous nature to loyal friends.

Enclosed documents catalogued by a local historian.

Document SP-JC 0001

Dated

Gutenberg Press 8th May 1782

Letter from Johann Carolus to his messenger.

Go at once and find out what strange events unfold at Salt Marsh House. I have reason to believe its noble heir, my own friend—Corvin Goldi is in great danger. He writes he has been stricken with a mysterious illness.

Write directly as the freedom of a great place depends on it and if as I fear it is true we will alert our good citizens to the invisible dangers that surround them. We can find the cause and advise a cure. Great times are upon us. We must be busy in our business and the business of God.

Letter from Ana Stutzman to her husband.

To Romain Stutzman

Strasbourg

8th May

Dearest Romain,

I think you should come back as soon as you safely can. Something is not right here and the more I read about the house, the more disturbing I find it.

Our friend, the journalist, bitterly regrets that society article and warns me daily. I don't want to write down what he says. It's horrible and in writing it down in deadly black and white makes it more real.

Please come home Romain, I miss you and I am afraid.

My love always,

Ana

Letter from Ana Stutzman to the Journalist.

C/O the Star Offices

14th May

Dear Friend,

It's so late and I have had no word of Romain and although I have asked in the town and paid good money to get messages I have no news of him.

The people stare at me from their fractured homes. I do not know if they are mad or me. Have you heard anything? Please let me know if you have. He wrote two days ago that he was setting out for Salt Marsh House. We are only 20 miles from the city.

I regret the day we began to research this House's history and sending him to that wretched library. We cannot hide in the past when the present is so fearful.

You must have some news surely? Something to tell me?

I don't know which is worse. The dumb silence or killing word.

Letter from the Journalist to Ana Stutzman

To: Ana Stutzman

SALT MARSH HOUSE

15TH May

I will do what I can dear Ana,

But you see for yourself the horrors that afflict this town. There is war and rumours of war. People are lost every day; they and the town are unrecognisable now.

Ana—is there anywhere safe you can go? Do you have friends nearby?

Please leave if you can. If I find Romain, I will let him know where you are.

Your friend.

•▬ ▬• •▬

Commander Ebb stopped reading, he was so close, he thought and yet nothing is real. Even the fragrance had vanished.

This beautiful, seemingly insubstantial room, he felt, would destroy all who sought sanctuary in it. A blind nightmare was rising out of the house and walking towards him. It was reaching for Commander Ebb with outstretched, sweeping arms and neither lightness nor darkness could prevent its touch.

The moon started to rise and Salt Marsh House was filled with the sound of birds shouting against the darkness, protecting their territories, chanting against strangers.

Singing the same song, through the centuries, across the marshes, through the grasses and the long day's eye, the watching Mere Hag heard their voices and began to stir. She reached out towards the house and began to draw it towards her.

Word by word she began to chant the mystery of Salt Marsh House, from the first sound it sent to her and the last.

The darkening house reflected her story, her words shimmering across its green shadowed walls as fish swimming through reeds.

The evening air floated through the window to Commander Ebb, rousing him, fighting off superstition. He called to the Private for more food and while waiting he stood up, took some papers and began walking through the house, reading their contents out loud; his voice filling the empty rooms, repeating the song of the Mere Hag, unknowing.

Night

.- -. .-

Photostat copy of newspaper edited by Johann Carolus – newspaper proprietor Strasbourg

Commander Ebb's grasp of language allowed him to translate clumsily

Account of all distinguished and commemorable news

Relation:

Aller Fürnemmen, vnd gedenckwürdigen Historien / so sich hin vnnd wider in Hoch vnnd Nieder Teutschland / auch in Franckreich / Italien / Schott vnd Engelland / Hispanien / Hungern / Polen / Siebenbürgen / Wallachey / Moldaw / Türckey / ꝛc. Inn diesem Jahr verlauffen vnd zutragen möchte.

Alles auff das trewlichst wie ich solche bekommen vnd zu wegen bringen mag / in Truck verfertigen will.

Heir of Salt Marsh House Brought Down by Witchcraft

The noble son of a great house is gravely ill and bears a terrible sickness. Corvin Goldi was found yesterday, collapsed in the grounds of Salt Marsh House. His faithful horse was standing by him. He cannot utter a word but spits out needles from his body. His tongue is pierced by them. His fear is dreadful to see and his priest prays for him. Corvin Goldi lies under enchantment but his bewitched father cannot see the evil that lies close to his hand. Around the house the cattle are dying and crops are failing. All the land turned to hard iron and the people say in the marshes the White Lady is walking again and visits Ana Goldi, the new wife of Salt Marsh House.

Who is she, ask the people, and what brought Ana to the house? Where has she come from and how did she charm the old man to a marriage bed? 'Nothing good has come to the house since she crossed its threshold,' said a servant of the place. Some others think she is the daughter of the marsh itself and is the end of days.

The priest who is at the bedside spoke of his horror at seeing the needles falling from the good son's mouth.

'God has forgotten Salt Marsh House,' the priest said, 'and will do while that woman lives.'

Night

Letter from Ana Stutzman to Romain her husband
20th May

Page One

Dearest Romain,

I know you are dead but I still write to you in this book for you to read. For you to know you are not forgotten and that you are loved. I love you Romain.

Dearest Romain, please forgive me; I fear that in sending you to find the story of our other, beloved Ana, I sent you to your death. But who could blame us Romain?

We were charmed by sweet Ana Goldi and wanted to rescue her out of her past. She was so brave and so young.

We couldn't see her danger was our own.

We all need Justice, Romain. We will have it. **I SWEAR IT!**

I pray every day to Our Lady, though I never prayed before.

The treacherous documents you sent from Strasbourg reached me securely, even if you did not.

It has taken a while to work

through the papers, darling. I sorted them into sections while I waited for you. I followed your instructions to the letter. I have categorised them and cross referenced with the little books we found in the library. The journalist has filled in additional information where the archives have faltered.

From them I began to put together the scattered pieces. This is what I have found. Once you have read them and I know you are happy, I will leave this house. There is nothing here anymore.

Night

'But you didn't leave, Ana,' Commander Ebb spoke aloud. 'You remain here with the house, casting on the horror to those that follow.' His wanderings had brought him back to the secret room and he continued to read. Moonlight by now was flooding across the paper, rendering the lamps that had been lit earlier, redundant.

He read the historical note the Journalist had sent to Ana Stutzman.

The Star: believed to have carried children and goods from Britain to mainland Europe and around the Mediterranean.

At the time, there was already a thriving trade in children in these regions. The archives are quite extensive and historians now believe the practice was widespread within Europe.

Generally, children were given up when families broke down. Often the death of a mother meant the father could not continue to work and look after any children. In these cases, they were sent at young ages to work out in the remote farm lands or the big houses such as Salt Marsh. Sometimes the religious orders took them and in these cases children were often shipped beyond the continent from Britain or Ireland. Over time the trade in children developed and became profitable. They could be worked hard for little overheads and were disposable labour.

Ana Stutzman continued her letter to her dead husband, her calm looping letters threading the known facts together.

Night

20th May

Page Two

Dearest Romain, I think Ana Goldi was brought by The Star as a trafficked child, but probably not intended to stay at the house long. The maid confirms this, although her word 'sent' has put an otherworldly tinge on the story.

A secret trader may explain Corvin's unexpected birth. Ana Goldi tells us an old man brought her to the house (from the boat presumably).

Night

Reading this now I wonder, from a child's point of view if it was a very old man of at least 30 years!

Ana Goldi was legally married to William Goldi. I have a copy of the marriage certificate which gives her age as 16.

In the fragments we have of her writing she appears to be a charming, observant child. She won over Corvin's aunt, her future sister in law. That lady of course would have no great love for Corvin and may have promoted Ana

Goldi's marriage as a way of getting a legitimate, unquestioned heir for her brother.

Ana Goldi and I love gardens; she is my cherished green girl. I kiss her on Time's bridge. I have found some household accounts that suggest Ana Goldi took more interest in plants than we first realised. She has signed off purchases for roses in the year of her marriage and complete lists of medicinal plants have been added in her hand at about the same time. All so *hopeful and yet she ended her days here in a secret room, listening—as I do now Romain.*

The sound of heavy footsteps moves through empty halls to this my occupied space and you cannot help me as they draw near.

The letter broke off suddenly, as if the writer had been interrupted. The handwriting ceased half way down a blank sheet.

. – – . . –

Commander Ebb stood up and looked around the room. Through the open door at the end of a long corridor he could see the Private, making his way towards him, staggering slightly as if on board a ship or drunk. Commander Ebb stepped back from the threshold; he wanted to leave but could not. He felt suddenly, absurdly as if he were waiting for news. A creeping dread began to overtake him. He turned and viewed his face in one of the room's pretty mirrors. He turned up his collar and flattened down his lapel. He looked back into the eyes of his reflection. 'I know the news.' He spoke out loud to the glass. 'The battle was won, but the war is lost'. His reflection answered him, causing him to straighten his back. 'You did not lose. You fought and you won. Honour at all times; even now when the days of your life are ending.' This was not the news he did not know. This was not horror. This he understood.

The sound of his voice steadied him.

Still standing he leaned over the table and uncovered a small handwritten card. The little, light action detonated a nail bomb, the sharp words exploding like so many needles, piercing his heart, stabbing his brain. Their tiny, steel lances entered his eyes, fixing their lids open, pinning him in place—transfixed.

EVERYBODY
KNOWS

Commander Ebb turned over the tiny postcard – the shock of recognition causing his breathing to become erratic, his heart to race and the scented air of the room began to choke him. The familiar taunting letters that he had killed off so many years ago, were living in this place and screaming at him.

Sir,
After much thought and many deliberations, I think you should know.
That child is not of your father's making.
Your mother plays him false and the baby calls cuckoo,
I write with honour and remind you of yours.

A Concerned friend.

The scarlet letter S dropped through the lines, shouting out Sin and Shame. Branding him, the pain searing him once again after all this time. Commander Ebb grasped the table to support himself. His head and neck hung beneath the yoke of his shoulders. The knotted muscles of his arms rode down to meet his long strong fingers that groped for an impossible solution to what lay beneath his hand. Striking, twisting and choking.

The Private entered the room. The bruises around his neck were turning purple and green. His bruised eyes were struggling to see. He was striking a match and lit a cigarette as he came in. He stumbled slightly as if his feet were numb. The smoke swirled around his face degrading it. For one moment Commander Ebb wondered who it was he saw.

'No news,' said the Private. Commander Ebb debated if this was a statement or question—

so flat was the tone of voice that the Private used.

'Not yet,' the Commander replied. After his shock, this brief exchange restored a military order. No unexpected horror had entered the room. Commander Ebb turned to look out of the window. The Private lurched up beside him. His cheek so close to the Commander's that he could smell the damaged skin. They both could see figures of men lined up at the edge of the grounds.

'They think we have mined the house, Sir,' said the Private. He seemed to be struggling to get the words out, gasping for breath. 'That's why they are waiting'. He turned to face his Commander and gave a strange smile. 'They may be right. Violence and fire solves everything in the end, doesn't it?'

He drew again on the cigarette, its tiny point glowing in the casement's shadow. 'Have you found what you've been looking for?' He glanced at the letters on the table, the postcard hastily hidden from sight, and then he said gently. 'All this time *reading* and still you haven't understood have you! All those letters and still no knowledge. Poor boy, you can't believe everything you read.'

The Private seemed to laugh but could not. Just a rattle. 'Read on,' he told Commander Ebb who was standing, gazing at him in an appalled suspicion.

'Did you? —are you?' he asked the Private.

But the Private fell to his knees looking up at him exhausted. 'My boy, I was never educated to read, to write—what good is reading to me in my place? Who looks for education here? You were the clever one, who understood all things. As you believed the first—will you believe the second?'

With an enormous effort of will the Private regained his feet and made a small salute. Then he turned to leave. As he gained the threshold Commander Ebb started after him but the Private turned. 'I will not see you again Sir,' he said simply. 'Everything you look for is in this room. This will be ended.' He shut the door and the Commander heard him put back some of the shelves that had previously hidden the room. Then a sudden stumble, a fall and no more.

Silence settled on Commander Ebb. The moon was full and flooded the room with its glow. The tapestries gleamed in the pale light. Sheep and shepherds flickered through the green forests and birds and angels sang in the high tree tops. In a daze Commander Ebb followed their journey under the starlight until they came upon a forest glade and a Virgin holding a child. Adored, glorified, beloved.

The gentleness of the Christmas scene took him unlooked for back to his childhood and the tenderness of his mother. The mother whom he had loved and the mother whom he—

Commander Ebb turned his back on the tapestries. The mother that had brought his family to such disgusting shame would not spend the last of his days with him now. He took a lamp to the table, sat down and thrusting the hateful card out of his way, took the next letter from Ana Stutzman and began to read.

.- -. .-

Letter from Ana Stutzman to the Journalist

C/O the Star Office

6th May

Page One

Dear Friend,

You asked me if I had found any more information about Ana Goldi and I have!

She was a gentle child of this house, a little Cinderella who grew up to marry a king. Clever and quick, she designed and stitched the tapestries that hang in the house. Her studies of plants and flowers hung here until recently; they are so beautiful.

Ana Goldi's household accounts are full of receipts for plants ordered for the garden. Each one known for either its beauty or its healing powers. Part of the garden was given over to herbs for cooking and medical use.

I know this as I found a ledger full of recipes and gardening notes.

I know it, thought Commander Ebb, —*that little book, lifeless in the library. I didn't read it carefully enough.* The 'something' that the Private had first noticed returned again to his face as he continued to read.

C/O the Star Office

Page Two

The ledger is regular in its updates—lavender to replace older shrubs, Damask roses are regularly imported and tulip bulbs in their hundreds were planted despite the salt air.

It would have been so beautiful and fragrant, as I read, the garden flowers again.

Anyway, the garden ledger is regular and uniform until shortly before Ana Goldi's arrest. The last entry is completely different.

An order is placed for a large quantity of Arnica and against the record a signature that looks like Corvin's.

This made me so curious I looked this plant up. It kills more readily than it cures: its common name is Leopard's Bane.

I do not believe that Ana Goldi's husband died naturally and I do not believe that Ana Goldi played any part in it.

It was Ana's stepson, Corvin, who used her good work and her strengths against her. Her end haunts me with this house. This beautiful, peaceful and elegant home that people have killed to keep.

As I begin to unpick this house's

history I find I am spun elsewhere. There are repeating patterns but nothing is the same.

I am alone and, like my other Ana; do not know how to leave. I don't expect a reply my friend. I doubt this letter will ever be sent or read.

Two pages from a botanical reference book and a pressed flower had been roughly glued to the page

Family: Asteracaea

Names : Arnica, Leopard's Bane

Night

Botanical description: A 20-30 cm tall perennial herb with opposite leaves.

1-3 flower-heads, one terminal and the others arising from the axils of the leaves. Receptacles 5-8 cm broad, with 15-25 yellow, ligulate florets.

Habitat : Native to Europe, Siberia and North West N. America.

Collection : The flowers are collected between June and August.

Part Used : Flower heads.

Indications:

For topical use only on unbroken skin,

Arnica should not be taken internally, nor applied to unbroken skin, The sesquiterpenes in Arnica are toxic to mammals. Toxicity symptoms include dizziness, trembling, diarrhoea, tachycardia or bradycardia, arrhythmias, hypertension, muscular weakness, dyspnoea, and collapse. Arnica poisoning can cause death due to circulatory paralysis with secondary respiratory arrest.

The sesquiterpene lactones are toxic causing gastroenteritis and with higher doses cardiac arrest. Helenalin is known to interfere with myocardial recovery in between contractions.

Two fluid ounces of its tincture has produced death.

•— —• •—

Letter from Ana Goldi.

SALT MARSH HOUSE

15th June 1782

This is my last letter. This is my last record.

I can hear the footsteps of men drawing to this room, I know I am alone. Who can help me now?

My dear husband left me here. This morning he left me with a kiss on my cheek. 'Sweetheart,' he said, 'stay here and do not worry. All will be well.' Then he went out and closed the door behind him. But he did not return. I heard a commotion in the house. So I too opened the door and stepped out.

It is summer outside. In the garden I could see my roses, the blue scented lavender and my neat rows of knotted hedge, growing like a charm. Something is flowering. It is a jarring yellow against the grass. I stare at it and wonder from whence this abundant gold has came. I do not, I realise, understand the garden. In so short a time, all has changed.

Night

I am wearing my silk, teal coloured dress and on it I have embroidered all the grasses that grow in the marsh. They drift over my growing stomach, whispering to the child who is sleeping. I walk through the hall to the great door. Eight years ago I came to the house and stood in rags and skin. Now I am clothed in flesh and silk. I rustle through the house.

I am calling 'William' and looking for my husband. He who took me for his own true wife, who took me for my youth, who grew great on me and gave me his child.

A man who can stop the natural order of things.

A man who took a servant and made her his wife—my lovely William Goldi. When he was young he took an old, rich wife and now being old he took me, a young and poor one. The treasure I have is his child in my body.

I find him eventually. My husband! William

Goldi. He has eaten. He has drunk. On the table I can see his meal, some bread, some broth, only a fingerful of amber liquid remains in his treasured crystal wine glass.

His eyes meet mine. They are wide open and staring. His head has fallen against the low chair back. His mouth is on top. His mouth hangs open. He is silent. Everything is silent.

The servants move towards him appalled, but someone darts between them and my poor man. Quick as a bird he claws at my husband's heart and then his wrist. The man looks up. I can see his flint grey eyes are full of words. He says three.

'He is dead.' Then he says two more. He gestures at me with a clenched fist. 'Look here.'

His fist flies open. Needles drop, falling and clanging on the flagstone floor. Their iron nature singing on the ground.

They were none of mine I noticed mutely. They

were crude things, made by a village blacksmith for peasant clothing.

For my dear man brought me a modern set of steel—as precious to me as his crystal wine cups to him. My needles' pricking surfaces were as smooth as glass, their points final. With these I had worked, as an artist, the finest textures. Representing in wool and silk the beauty of the world. With my steel needles and my silks, I worked living plants and breathing beasts. They waxed under the sunshine of golden threads and lived merrily as we all did then. But my embroideries cannot speak for me now. They cannot reach out and slip me into a woven world where I may be safe.

The iron needles on the floor appal me. I step back. A hushed horror runs around the room. The servants flock together, blocking my exit from the house. The birdlike man springs to my table and from his jacket brings some paper. He plucks some charcoal *from the dead fire. Rapidly he scratches his words down, committing to paper things that are and are not.*

'I, Johann Carolus, before God have witnessed an unnatural death this day. My suspicions are great and press upon me. Dear friend contact the justices and good people of Strasbourg. Bring them immediately to Salt Marsh House. No time must be lost or else we will all perish and the witch's child will rule here.'

The message is read aloud whilst the servants avert their eyes from me. I want to run to the marshes and the star from where I believe I came. But they hold out their hands against me. I move through the house. Wordlessly, they follow. I visit each room as if for the last time but am not allowed to sit or rest. Finally I reach this confined space again and here I can go no further and with its small windows they allow me to remain.

Night

I knew no sentence I could find would stop the words uttered against me. As I cannot sew, I will write and then I will hide. When my husband saw at last the danger in the rumours, he died. But not by me. I needed him for me to grow and thrive.

I hear the horses galloping up the drive, I hear the cast of forged iron on stone, I hear the men's' voices as they near this door.

I am Ana and have done none harm.

Letter to Roman Stutzman from Ana Stutzman.
To Romain Stutzman
15th June
Page One

Dear Romain,

I can't speak of what happened to me. I turn to our local history and my sweet friend Ana Goldi for comfort and find none. You left me my dear husband. You did not come back.

Salt Marsh House lies here, breathing still. Its heart has only one beat. I can hear it now. I recognise its pattern.

.- -. .- .- -. .- .- -. .- .- -. .- .- -. .- .- -. .- .- -.
.- .- -. .- .- -. .- .- -. .- .- -. .-

I am going to tell you , sweet man, what the good men of Strasbourg did to our Ana. Then I will tell you what they did to me. Then you can tell me dear Romain why you didn't stop them. You can explain , my dear Romain, why the men don't stop?

Commander Ebb was unmoved by her question. 'We don't stop,' he muttered, 'because, on the whole, we don't have to.' He read on.

To Romain Stutzman

15th June

Page Two

They took Ana Goldi from this room where I sit now. Poor child. She must have hidden her little document in a book that was eventually returned to the great library unread—like all the books here! Why didn't we read them Romain?—Why didn't we learn? You brought me to this house for your dream and like a fool I followed you. You killed me with your hope. The Goldis killed Ana. Her husband was blind too. Corvin was not. He took her. He killed her. He got his way.

She was sixteen and a child. She

took one of her tapestries and put it over this little table. Where I am reading. Where I am writing, in the room that I found when nothing was safe anymore. The great folds reached the carpeted floor. She had worked that cloth well. Ana Goldi had covered it with the plants from the marsh and the great house.

There is a virgin, there is a child. There are useless shepherds who do not see the wolves at hand. All are transfixed by an illusion. Each charmed by hope and love as we were. All the creatures of the land are included in the tapestries.

Spiders hang from their silken

webs, flies crawl on water, a toad hops amongst the meadow flowers. I look at this tapestry now. I should have read it better. I should have understood more.

For I know, Romain, these pictures fit us for nothing. The warp and the weft, Romain, do not connect us as we hope. Why did you not see it? We are rent. Why did you bring us here to our death and to our ruin?

When Ana Goldi had laid the table, she crawled on her hands and knees and hid under it.

The good men of Strasbourg enter the room and believe her to be gone. They tell each other she turned into a raven and flew away—up the chimney.

They can hear her calling and screeching in the reeds and the marsh.

But Johann Carolus enters the room; he cocks his head to one side. His gaze flits about the place. He observes a tiny fragment of teal silk, shimmering against some wool cloth. The poor duck. He bends down and lifts the cover. His eye spies her. He thrusts in his black clad arm and claws Ana out.

She is sixteen. She is pregnant. She is weeping.

'Behold, the witch.' he says.

It is midsummer.

The good men of Strasbourg make light work of Ana and her denials. The long evenings give them sufficient time.

Night

She refuses she is a witch. She refuses she charmed Mr. Goldi into a wicked marriage and his death. She refuses all knowledge of Corvin and his strange sickness. She refuses it all.

So this is what they do to her—our Ana Goldi. They held her down and tied her hands behind her back. Then they hoisted her up by a rope and pulley by her shoulders. Stone weights were tied to her ankles to increase the pain.

Under these conditions, Ana finally broke and confessed to having formed a pact with Satan and his hag. Once the torture had ceased, her child miscarried. Anna recanted her confession, but it was too late.

Night

Anna Goldi was put on trial and she was found guilty.

She was sentenced to death by beheading.

The sentence was carried out the same day—June 18.

Johann Carolus watched her trial. He watched her die. He carolled her story. He crowed her news. This is what he said. This is what he printed. These were his sentences.

Yet God is Good

18th June 1782

Now to speake a few words more of one great mercy of God, in that he hath brought to light the witch and hath justice to be executed on her here.

Anna Goldi imprisoned in the town by the testimony of the town and without any forcing or compulsion freely declares that she has made a covenant with the Devill and the Mere Hag, to forsake God and Christ, and to take Satan as her master.

Likewise she do acknowledge that divers Cattells and som Christians have been killed by her means. Others lie sick unto death.

This was certified from some that were with her, with other particulars which would not have been believed had not many, including this writer of the town, seen and observed them. By this wee may see the grand delusions and impostures of Satan by which he works upon men and women in these latter times of the world. What sins so hanious what crimes so grevious will not women run into once God is gone?

Ana Stutzman continued her account.

Johann Carolus wrote his memoirs and kept the presses running night and day. The street sellers sold old ballads with Ana Goldi's name on it. Her teal dress was cut up and marketed as souvenirs. Her servants grew fat on free beer and cakes as they spoke of her in public houses. Any second-hand needle for a while was sold as hers.

She was a child with child, Romain, and they killed her. Others died also? What of me? —Woman, not hag, Fertile, not mother, widow, not wife? Where fit I? Who will save me?'

I will save you, decided Commander Ebb. He paused. He read on. Ana Stutzman continued.

Someone writes that they will save

me. It is not the journalist. The journalist is silent. It is not our good friends of the town. The mystery writer cannot save me. I can save me, but I will not save him.

They hid all the documents relating to Ana Goldi, Romain. I am sure of it. The archivist hit on the truth when he said the records must have been deliberately misfiled. No one is comfortable with her history. To this day, no one will speak of it.

Johann Carolus set up a great house in Strasbourg's fine Square—far beyond any income that he could earn—even though his presses worked night and day. Corvin inherited Salt

Marsh House. He recovered the day Ana died, to no-one's real surprise. The people held on to the witch words, but their private true minds worked out the reality.

When Corvin inherited the house and all its possessions he had the family coat of arms changed.

He never explained the leopards dancing on the green plant or the star struck out. Now when I gaze around the house I see its emblem everywhere. Where once I saw history and *pageantry, I see darkness.*

Corvin Goldi lived a long life and died peacefully in his bed.

But the old bones of the house knew its history and it could be read by anyone with an eye. It writes its story in stone and paper. It writes with charcoal and pen. It is still writing. It is repeating its history. We walk in its doors and become like so many blank pages to be written on. We are bound between the house's boards, stitched into its spine, its back, its very walls.

I leave out paper and find writing that is not mine on them. Sometimes I think I see the Mere Hag, in the corridors and in the halls. She knows our history. She does not forget. She does not forgive. She does not rest. In the reeds and in the marshes she sings the truth to those that will hear.

There are new letters that tell the same tale—but not mine and not poor Ana Goldi's either. They are addressed to someone else. A different Ana. Flowing and frightening letters tell the same story with similar end.

I wonder who can escape from this house. I want to crawl under the table, pull the tapestries around my ears and hide.

Your poor wife Ana x

·– –· ·–

The familiar handwriting stopped. There were no more letters from Ana Stutzman.

I must know, thought Commander Ebb feverishly, *where is she? What has she become?*

He gazed at the blocked door. The feeling grew on him again that if he could open the door in *this second of time, in this second way*. It would open, it must open and it had to open on another different room, where Ana would be.

In his mind he broke down the door but there in that other hidden chamber he saw his mother standing. Surrounded by sunlight. Surrounded by high summer. Rising to face him, the child in her arms, smiling, holding out the baby for him to admire, for him to adore. His brother whom he could love but should not; for he had reason. He had word. He thrust the black birded card at his mother.

Night

EVERYBODY
KNOWS..

Sir,
After much thought and many deliberations, I think you should know.
That child is not of your father's making.
Your mother plays him false and the baby calls cuckoo.
I write with honour and remind you of yours.
A Concerned friend.

Night

Ana Ebb 18th June

She pleading. She pitching to her knees. She cannot read. She cannot understand the messages against her. 'S' shimmering its reflection in the mirror behind her. She, not breathing - his fingers and the Scarlet card at her throat, her hair flying; the child falling from her hands. Son

doing what his father Should.
Son Seeing what had to be
done. Sin Stopped.
Honour plucked out from
diShonour.

Peace. Rest. Silence. Sleep.

.- -. .-

Charles Ebb, Commander, had risen from his mother's fragile, broken room. He turned at its threshold. He struck a match and set it to the delicate materials, the lavender bags and fragrant perfumed oils. He shut the door carefully behind him. He made his way, slowly down the stairs and out into the gardens and walked with his father amongst the scented flowers.

His father spoke with him of love and joy in new life, his honoured mother. He laughed. His father turned. His father looked up and saw the smoke and the flames seek out from the high windows; leaping to join the sun in the bright day.

Publicly, it was said — despite the hot summer — a candle perhaps or a fire spark; a terrible accident. But privately, his father regarded his son and his eyes burned in his head.

In this room, as through a mirror, Commander Ebb saw all this reflected clearly. The death of his mother. As it was. As it had happened. As he had killed her. As in fact, there had been nothing else to do, under the circumstances.

But this was not the something that he sensed was on its way to destroy him. A nameless thing was walking through the marshes, gardens and rooms of Salt Marsh House to halt at the door in front of him. Waiting and breathing. He could hear whispers of things that were not. He saw glimpses of things that were not. A final door would open in his mind and tell him things that that he knew not, that were not and could not be. That door remained shut fast. In his mind he barricaded this door against the private, secret things that were hastening towards it. That wanted to throw it open and speak.

He could smell their sweet perfumes; he could hear their rustling silks. In the darkness outside, he heard a child cry.

She rises with the moon, the Mere Hag. She is full and in beauty. She rises from the silken reeds and the green. She flows from the water, her grey dress liquefying on her, shimmering. Insects climb and stick stitch themselves into the fabric as she moves from the marshes. She breathes in the fragrant starlit air. She reaches out and plucks white moon-flowers from the garden of Salt Marsh House. She stretches out her long fingers and night flying moths settle on them. A great star rises over her head. She gazes on Salt Marsh House and its fine white stone. The frame of the house moves with her, settling. She smiling enters her house in richness.

The Mere Hag speaks through the darkened halls, the moonlight shining on floors, she raises the dust as it floats in the silver light, solidifying, taking form, the bones write, the ashes whisper.

'Ana,' she says. 'Ana.' The name rings

through the house. 'Speak now at last my last Ana.'

Commander Ebb can hear her. He puts his hands to his ears. The moonlit room is spinning round him. The final door unshutting. In his mind he puts his weight against the timbers. He pushes back.

The voices of Ana whisper through the cracks, the sound travelling through the keyhole, crawling under the door, rising from the floorboards.

'Where is he?' they are calling. 'Where are you? We are coming to get you,' and laughter. As though he were a child, as though it were a game of hide and seek. Which it is, Commander Ebb, suddenly realises. Except he is not the seeker.

The horror takes one step towards him. He is not what he thought. Fear grips his throat. He is in hiding. Knowing he is hidden, knowing he is in darkness, but not hidden enough, not in darkness enough. Not now. Knowing that the seekers know where to look, as they always do in the end, the secret room of the mind.

He believes the Mere Hag is at his door and he breathes in, feels her sharp night air. He hears her breathing, then one more voice that thrills him. It speaks clearly. He watches the door motionless. 'There he is,' says a woman's voice. 'My son!' Commander Ebb falls to his knees. He is pressing the door shut in his mind. But through the secret door in Salt Marsh House he sees eyes gleaming at him. He hears the third and last voice talking to him; his mother—his mother, Ana. But this can't be for she is dead and he has killed her. He closes his eyes with the heels of his hands and rocks on his knees.

'You do not listen, my boy?' Her voice steel and cold as it never used to be. She continues, 'You never did!' Commander Ebb began to choke. His throat closing in terror as her words continued, ripping out the tacks that held him together. 'Nothing I could say could reach you. Only black on white taught you. Closing you down with their printed strokes. Surrounding you like bars. Fencing you in. Binding you in the established ways. Not straying, not thinking. Moving like an automaton from black to white. Switching you steaming, down narrow and mistaken tracks. You were coded and you were branded. You did not hear me; you would not see me soI have this, this last letter.

'unpin your eyes, my son, and read!'

Her voice stopped. Commander Ebb collapsed and lay with stretched out arms, out across the floor. His hands palm down on the patterned carpet. A sharp scent reached him—of darkness, the stench of marsh water and fell reeds, long rotted, long ended. All dead. Commander Ebb moaned and drew himself up onto his hands and knees. His straying fingers felt, before his eyes saw, a final sheet of paper, lying hidden under the table. The sealed door in his mind burst open and a final torrent rushed the nameless terror to his transformed and woken senses.

Memory returned him to his father's study, after the funeral. He saw a letter lying face up, abandoned on a pile of news cuttings and notes of condolences. The page, translucent as though long soaked in water, the writing faint and obscure in a brownish green ink. He realised, as he traced the dull letters through the soaking paper, that it was addressed to his lost father.

RICHARD,

I SENT THEM. I SENT THE CARDS. I SENT THEM TO YOU—BUT YOU BURNT THEM AND LAUGHED AT ME. YOU KNEW YOUR FAITHFUL, TRUE WIFE BETTER THAN YOUR SON DID. SO I SENT THEM TO CHARLES, YOUR SWEET BOY—THAT HONOUR CODED INNOCENT. I SENT SO MANY, MY BLACK AND HATE FILLED CARDS. I LOST COUNT OF WHAT I SENT. I PLACED THEM EVERYWHERE HE WOULD FIND THEM. HE READ THEM AND

HE BELIEVED. CHARLES, YOUR SON, DID MORE THAN I DARED IMAGINE.

MY PASSION FOR YOU MADE ME JEALOUS AND JEALOUSY MADE ME MAD. I THOUGHT IF ANA WOULD JUST GO AWAY, IF SHE COULD BE DRIVEN OUT, THEN YOU WOULD FINALLY BE FREE TO MARRY ME AND WE COULD BE HAPPY.

Commander ebb could read no more now, no more now than he could then. The door that had been slammed shut was now wide opened upon his slandered, innocent mother.

Commander Ebb staggered to his feet. He could hear sobbing and realised it was he, weeping, clutching the green stained paper to his chest. The walls of the darkening room seemed to creep towards him. All was the same, yet all was unfastened, all was unwrapping around him.

He heard rather than saw a door unlock and there in the hidden room stood Ana Stutzman. She regarded him steadily.

She beckoned to Commander Ebb who followed her, speechless. Entering the great hall, he saw the body of the private lying where he had fallen and with a dull recognition Commander Ebb realised he had been dead for some days.

Ana walked past the body, seemingly

unmoved; she paused at the entrance of Salt Marsh House.

Commander Ebb clutched at the threshold's carved stonework. His fingers strayed blindly across the doorway's intricate and finely chiseled symbols.

Commander Ebb turned desperately to Ana Stutzman, but she forestalled him.

'You are dishonour,' she said,' either within your code or without it.'

'Ana!' but he could say no more. He was unstrung, words spilled out of his mouth, unraveled across the floor. With one swift movement Ana Stutzman reeled his sentences in, wound them up and cut them off.

'There are no words left,' she said. 'their work is done. Justice is here.'

Commander Ebb passed out through the door of Salt Marsh House towards the line of men waiting in the distance. Those silent watchers saw a man stagger towards them and from their low angle it seemed that, when he raised his arms upright in surrender, his long fingers pierced the fabric of the sky and icy stars that hung above them.

- .... .   . -. -..

The End

Author's Note:

Salt Marsh House has roots in the history of Alsace, It is set, of course, in a fictional Strasbourg-On-Sea

However, if you visit the villages outside Strasbourg, you will find many synagogues now being used as private residences.

The Jews had been expelled along with non-German speaking Alsatians in 1870 German-Franco war. Later, all but the Jews were permitted to return.

I wondered how a house would behave if it were repurposed and reoccupied by people who had no understanding of its history.

Appendices

Character details

Name	Imagined	Biographical Notes	Font
SALT MARSH HOUSE	Yes & No	As well as the shared roots with Alsace there is a strong association with Pallant House Gallery in Chichester. Pallant House was rescued from debt in the 18th Century by an owner who married a wealthy widow. His sister did beg him on her knees not to marry her and the marriage was scandalously unhappy. The house has its very own slippery dark staircase. This writer could not tell you one thing about any of the paintings in this gallery. She was completely captivated by this brief museum account of the house's history.	Calibri 12
Commander Ebb	Yes	Is a man travelling under a curse He needed his story to be told. Probably has a root in the Bosnian Wars of the 1990s.	Rage Italic (He only writes once where the reader can see it. 'How?')
Ana Ebb	Yes	Commander Ebb's Mother	None specific to her

Richard Ebb	Yes	Commander Ebb's Father	None specific to him
Poison pen writer	Yes	Jealous and Mad	Blackmail Font & final letter in Chiller 22

Name	Imagined	Biographical Notes	Font
Ana Goldi	Yes & No	Anna Göldi, a 48-year-old servant in the house of prominent citizen Johann Jakob Tschudi, was convicted of "bewitching" the family's eight-year-old daughter, causing her to spit pins and have convulsions. Tschudi, a doctor and magistrate, apparently had sexual relations with Göldi, and his reputation would have been seriously damaged if the adultery became public. There is a museum to her memory in Mollus where she lived and the Canton of Glarus recognised in *2007* that she was falsely accused[1]. Anna Goldi fled to Strasbourg but was returned. A film has been made	Bradley Hand TC

1 www.swissinfo.ch/eng/politics/internal_affairs/Last_witch_to_be_declared_innocent.html?cid=662094 (Accessed September 17th 2012)

		of her life but the writer has not seen it. Completely fictionalised in **Salt Marsh House.**	
Elizabeth Goldi	Yes	None other than Pallant House notes	None specific to her.
William Goldi	Yes	None other than Pallant House notes	None specific to him
Corvin Goldi	Yes	None : motivated by greed	Century School Book 12

Name	Imagined	Biographical Notes	Font
Journalist	Yes	Both investigates and reveals information.	Courier 12
Johann Carolus	Yes & No	**Johann Carolus** (1575–1634) was a German publisher of the first newspaper, called *Relation aller Fürnemmen und gedenckwürdigen Historien* (Account of all distinguished and commemorable news). Lived and worked in Strasbourg. In **Salt Marsh House** he is a complete work of fiction. Friend to Corvin Goldi. The work **Yet God is Good** is adapted from 16th Century pamphlet- Tatton Park Notebook[2]. English Witchcraft Trials	Times Roman 12
Ana Stutzman	Yes	Wealthy and idealistic she is the only character who learns to read Salt Marsh House.	Lucida Handwriting 11
Romain Stutzman	Yes	Wealthy and idealistic. Starts to investigate **Salt Marsh House** but is unable to understand its dangers until too late.	Segoe Script 12
The Bagman	Yes	A thief; his clarity and kindness to Commander Ebb enable him to escape from the house.	None specific to him

2 http://www.manchester.ac.uk/aboutus/news/display/?id=6771 (accessed September 17th 2012)

Illustrations

Journalist's photo of marks on fireplace:	Image uncovered at Kew Palace: http://www.hrp.org.uk/evidenceofevilspirits
Ana Stutzman photo in Illustrated Life	Taken from a blog showing how to apply make up in 1940s style: http://zoerichardsphotography.blogspot.co.uk/2008/03/40s-themed-fashion-shoot.html (Accessed 17th September 2012)
Johann Carolus' newspaper: Account of all distinguished and commemorable news	Photocopy of original front page. The date has been edited out in **Salt Marsh House.**
Woodcut of enchanted Corvin Goldi - horse in background	By Hans Baldung born in 1484/85. The young Baldung may have received his earliest training around 1500 in the Upper Rhineland by an artist from Strasbourg, France. F http://arthistory.about.com/od/namesgg/l/bl_sp_grien.htm (Accessed September 17th 2012)
The Star - Engraved ship	Believed to be an engraving of the Star of India
Leopards Bane/Arnica (x2)	Wikimedia commons licence
Corvin Goldi's Arms	Adapted from the Somalia National flag
The poison pen letters	Taken from an online site on how to draw Crows/ravens. This has since disappeared.
Photo of French House	Writer's own.

Bibliography

Books that helped build **Salt Marsh House** (in order of priority)	How they helped.
Mantel Hilary, *Bring Up The Bodies,* (Fourth Estate; First Edition, 1st Printing edition 10 May 2012)	Mantel's characters inhabit a claustrophobic and enclosed world. Her characters inhabit, for the most part, small rooms and conduct intimate and intimidating conversations that impact in surprising ways upon the future. This writer found the distance between the reader and characters interesting and useful. E.g. Mantel refers to Cromwell in the third person '*he*' throughout.
Kennedy AL, *The Blue Book,* (Vintage; 2 Aug 2012)	The Blue Book plays with the book's physical structure, e.g. page numbers and explores the fate of two main characters that inhabit an artificially isolated environment. They are made to work through their shared history to a devastating conclusion
Klaus Theweleit, Male Fantasies: Women, Floods, Bodies, *History v. 1,* (Trans, Conway Stephen, Polity Press; Cambridge 1987) Copy in University of Winchester Library	This was read after Commander Ebb arrived. The writer had to stop writing for some time and think very carefully about who this man was, what he had done and why. This book helped the writer understand Ebb's background and consequently did not soften him as a result.
Richardson Samuel, *Clarissa or the history of a young lady,* (Penguin Classics; Reprint edition 29 Aug 1985)	The letter format allows short and long time spans. Emotions are read second hand. Technically, this writer was made aware that it was essential to date the letters in **Salt Marsh House.** Some letters in **Salt Marsh House** are written on the same day and month, if not the same year to mirror previous histories.
Shakespeare, William, *Shakespeare's Sonnets* , (A Public Domain Book - Kindle Edition)	Sonnet No X11: in order to study rhythm and structure of the sonnet form.
Gibbons Stella, *Cold Comfort Farm,* (Penguin Classics; Reprint edition 26 Oct 2006)	For reminding the writer that a sense of humour is essential when living with mad people.

Websites and quotes

Dekker Thomas, *The Wonderful Year:*
http:// www.luminarium.org/renascence-editions/yeare.html
(Accessed 17th September 2012: Contains the magical phrase: *rich men looke as pale as their white money* that the Bagman hears in **Salt Marsh House).**

Description of Leopards Bane: arnica Montana. doc
http:/www/aaronsworld.com
(Accessed September 25th 2012)

Morse code translation site:
http:// www.onlineconversion.com/morse_code.htm
(Accessed September 17th 2012)

Ana Goldi's quote, *'had I been born crested and not cloven,'* was said by Queen Elizabeth 1st to her councillors.

Printed in Great Britain
by Amazon

59654110R00119